MONSTER CLUB

CLUB
HUNTERS FOR HIRE

MONSTER CLUB

CLUB HUNTERS FOR HIRE

BY

GAVIN BROWN

SCHOLASTIC PRESS • NEW YORK

FOR GALEN, WHO FOUGHT GREMLINS
AND TROLLS WITH ME EVEN WHEN
HE WOULD RATHER HAVE BEEN
PLAYING AMERICAN REVOLUTION

Library of Congress Cataloging-in-Publication Data available

ISBN 978-1-338-31851-7

10 9 8 7 6 5 4 3 2 1   19 20 21 22 23

Printed in the U.S.A. 37
First edition, August 2019

Book design by Christopher Stengel

CHAPTER 1

TOMMY

Everyone in Ms. Jander's third-period science class jumped when the alarm buzzed and red-and-white lights started flashing above the door.

Tommy Wainwright tensed in his seat. Was this it—a real emergency? An opportunity to escape a deadly fire? Or an infestation of acidic toads they would need to battle their way through? Had Karim been right about the basilisk footprints he said he found? Tommy was ready for anything.

Principal Jackson's voice crackled over the intercom. "This is not a drill. Everyone please remain where you are. We will update you soon."

Tommy grinned at his friends Karim and Spike, who were sitting next to him at the back of the class. Karim looked scared, as usual, and Spike was just watching with a knowing smirk. They didn't get it. This could be their big chance to have something crazy awesome happen!

Suddenly, the flashing lights went dark. The classroom erupted with chatter, but Ms. Jander rapped her knuckles on her desk and the students fell mostly silent.

"I know you're all distracted, but we're not finished with class," she said. "We need to get through this week's unit on substances with mystical properties. The supernatural biology group presentations are just around the corner."

The class groaned in unison.

"Yesterday," Ms. Jander continued, "we covered mystical substances like sour ooze, which can expand from a small mass to a hundred times its original size. Last night's reading was on a different substance with mystical properties."

Tommy perked up when she mentioned "supernatural biology" and "sour ooze." Finally, they were talking about something *useful* in science class! Enough of this stuff about the water cycle and electricity; studying monsters was the only thing that could make school interesting.

"Tommy, did you do the reading last night?" Ms. Jander asked.

Perking up had clearly been a mistake. "Uh, yeah," Tommy said. It wasn't a total lie; he'd glanced at it when she handed it out. That counted for something, right?

Tommy didn't know why Ms. Jander called on him so much. Maybe it was how often he got distracted during class. Or it might be because Tommy was a head taller than most of the other seventh graders. He normally enjoyed looking like a giant among mere mortals, but it did seem to draw an unusual amount of attention from teachers—even if they often assumed he was a big idiot. Just because he was a big hunk of beefcake didn't mean he was a moron.

"Tommy, do you remember the difference between a meteoroid, a meteor, a meteorite, and meteorium?"

Tommy stared back blankly. Those words were all really similar. Why should there even *be* a difference?

"Well? It was in last night's reading." Ms. Jander didn't seem disappointed; she didn't expect Tommy to know the answer. But that didn't mean she was going to let him off the hook.

A lesser person would have stayed silent, or admitted to not knowing the answer. But that wasn't Tommy. No, Tommy never backed down from a challenge, no matter where it came from, no matter how ill-prepared he was. So what if he didn't have the answer in his head? Tommy might not be book smart, but at least he had guts. Maybe he was gut smart.

"Meteors are shooting stars." He knew that much was true. "And, um, meteoroids are people who are big fans of them. And meteorites are, like, people who shoot them down." Tommy nodded. He'd probably nailed it, just by listening to his gut.

"And meteorium?" Ms. Jander asked.

"Uh . . . that's when you grind up meteors and use it to season burgers." Tommy was pretty sure he'd seen that on *Now You're Cooking with Gas*, his favorite cooking show. Gaston Lefevre was both a great chef and totally ripped. "Mussels to build muscles" was an inspirational segment.

Ms. Jander stared at him for a moment. "Well, that's very . . . creative, Tommy," she said. "But sadly not the least bit correct. Does anyone want to help him out?"

Tommy sagged in his chair. Of course he'd gotten it wrong. Maybe he was just the big dumb lug everyone thought he was. Just because he started every morning with a Brotein ("The power to bro down and crush it") shake, that didn't make him dumb.

And now the whole class was staring at him. He could feel them judging him. He looked around, hoping that someone would bail him out, but no one else said a thing.

Ms. Jander focused her attention on someone else. "Karim, what about you?"

Karim shrunk back. "Um . . . meteorium is what you can make magical weapons out of." He sped up as he got started. "You have to forge it properly, usually with volcanic heat. Like my dad did in the episode when he needed a magical ballista bolt to defeat the—"

"Thank you," Ms. Jander interrupted him. "That's correct. Which is why meteorium is one of the most valuable substances on earth. It's the only thing that can harm most monsters."

That was actually pretty cool, Tommy had to admit. He resolved to do more than just glance at the reading next time.

"What about meteors, meteorites, and meteoroids?" Ms. Jander asked.

More silence. Tommy stared at his desk. Maybe he should

give his gut smarts another crack at it. Maybe they just needed to warm up first.

But then Spike sighed and spoke up. "Meteoroids are rocky bodies in space. A meteor is the streak of light we see in the sky when the meteoroid burns up in our atmosphere. And meteorites are just meteoroids after they land on Earth."

Ms. Jander nodded sharply. "There! That wasn't so hard, was it?"

"How did you know that?" Tommy whispered. It really wasn't like Spike to study any time there wasn't a test the next day.

Spike shrugged and pointed at the front of the room. It was all Tommy could do to keep from smacking himself on the forehead. The answer was already written on the board, probably from the last class. All he'd needed to do was look.

I wasn't made for this school stuff, he thought. *I was made for big adventures.*

That's when the alarm went off a second time.

Principal Jackson's voice boomed from a speaker on the wall. Most people looked up at the ceiling as if they were hearing the voice of God, but Spike knew better—she had once snuck into the office to make a fake announcement. The intercom was just a microphone still slightly sticky from someone spilling a drink on it years ago.

"Can I have your attention, please," the voice said. "A basilisk has been sighted in the school. All students and staff are to remain in their classrooms with the doors closed while an agent from the Burbank Monster Control Bureau handles the situation."

"I was right!" Karim whispered. The class hummed with a mix of excitement and fear.

Spike sighed. "Yeah, but this ruins our plan." From the moment Karim had spotted basilisk footprints in the dust under a radiator, they had been plotting to catch it themselves. "There's no way we can hunt it now. They'll have 'professionals'"—she said that last part with air quotes—"take care of it."

Monsters were all around, sure, and they'd seen a couple of Level 1 monsters in captivity at Adventure Camp, where they learned how to be adventurers and hunt monsters. But having a real Level 2 monster like a basilisk at their school seemed about as likely as a big movie star showing up in the cafeteria. They lived a half hour's drive from Hollywood, so it wasn't *totally* impossible. But yesterday the basilisk in the school had seemed like a fantasy. Suddenly, it was real.

"Are you saying I got that weasel fur for nothing?" Tommy asked. "That was *not* easy!"

"Yup," Spike answered, smiling. "Sorry." Their chance to hunt a monster was ruined, but the thought of Tommy somehow shaving a weasel—and it being completely pointless—did bring her some small consolation.

The class buzzed with speculation as a van with flashing lights rushed past the window.

"It's kind of a relief that monster control will be taking care of it, right?" Karim whispered as everyone ran to the window. "At least we know my footprint ID was right."

Ms. Jander tried to get the class back on track again, but it was a losing battle. Spike could've told her it was a total waste of time, but for the next ten minutes the teacher tried to lecture them about the moon's orbit. Still, the students were all fidgeting, checking their phones or peering out the windows, as if something interesting was happening.

It was almost starting to get funny to watch, when the

lights flashed and the principal's voice crackled on the loud-speaker again. "All students and staff are directed to follow the emergency exit signs and evacuate the building."

"What happened to monster control?" one student asked.

Spike scoffed and headed for the door.

Outside, the hallways were chaotic. Students pushed and shoved to get in front of one another. The normal order of fire drills had evaporated under the threat of a real monster.

As she was carried in the press of students, Spike whistled softly to Tommy and Karim. In a nook outside the art room, two students had been turned to stone—actual gray rock. The basilisk was no joke, though Spike knew the petrification effect would wear off eventually. Maria Struthers and Eddie Suarez had their arms wrapped around each other, and both were frozen looking down in shock, presumably where the basilisk had been when their eyes met.

"Looks like somebody was skipping class for a quick smooch!" Tommy said with glee.

Some students were giggling, but others looked scared.

Spike shrugged. "We don't have time to stand around and gawk. Now's our chance." This was their moment, and Spike was not about to let anything get in their way.

"Chance for what?" Karim asked.

These boys sure were thick. As the other students and teachers stared dumbfounded at the petrified kids, Spike pulled her friends out of the crowd and through a set of doors. She was going to lead them to victory, no matter what it took.

CHAPTER 3

KARIM

The three friends ducked underneath a staircase as students clomped down the stairs above them, ringing on the metal like a stampede of spike-horned ironhooves. Or, at least, what Karim imagined ironhooves would sound like if they ran down a flight of stairs. It didn't make sense, but that was the picture in his head. Which was pretty typical of the things that bounced around in there.

The trio stood still while the herd above them thinned to just a few footfalls, then silence.

"What are we doing?" Karim hissed. "You heard the announcement! We need to get out of here." He had a feeling Spike was about to get them all in big trouble. Again.

"Yeah, shouldn't we be going outside like the principal said?" Tommy said, speaking through a mouthful of protein bar.

"Or . . ." Spike grinned. "We have the weasel fur. We have the mirrored goggles. We were planning to hunt the basilisk after school, anyway."

"But now it's different!" Karim protested. "We're supposed to evacuate! And who knows what the basilisk did to the person from monster control!" This was typical Spike. Push them to go off on some stupid risky adventure with no thought for how bad things could get. "What if we get turned to stone?!"

"Well, it's not forever like when a medusa petrifies you, right?" Tommy said.

"Let's see what Mort's has to say," Karim huffed, pulling out his phone.

Mortimer's Monsterpedia was Karim's very favorite app. Of course, it hadn't always been an app. Whenever his dad went out of town on a business trip, Karim would sneak into the study and read the original print book—a massive tome filled with details on thousands of monsters.

The book detailed the strengths and weaknesses of every monster and even rated their level of danger on a scale from one to ten.

Nowadays, the app version of Monsterpedia had up-to-date info on all the known monsters, and they'd even added cool new features like a Monster-to-English translator.

It didn't take long for Karim to find the entry on basilisks. His friends might not believe him, but they would definitely believe Mortimer, even if Karim sometimes wondered just how reliable Mortimer's notes were.

BASILISK

LEVEL 2 MONSTER

The basilisk is a crested, four-legged reptile that can grow up to a foot in length. Basilisks don't look terribly threatening, but beware! Their gaze is dangerous. Direct eye contact can turn a hapless adventurer to stone.

HABITAT: Basilisks exist on several continents and can be found in any hot climate. They don't like large, open spaces and prefer to make their homes in warm caves, away from humans.

THREAT ANALYSIS: Direct eye contact with a basilisk will temporarily petrify humans. Common North American basilisks can turn a person to stone for only a few weeks, but there are rumors of ancient creatures whose petrifying effects last for months, years, or even all eternity (see also: *Medusa*).

WEAKNESSES: Basilisks can be killed only by weasels or powerful enchanted weapons. These reptiles are so scared of weasels that, if exposed to weasel fur, they will be temporarily paralyzed by sheer terror.

MORTIMER'S NOTES: I'll admit, one time I "accidentally" let myself get turned to stone by a basilisk to avoid a family reunion I really didn't want to attend.

"Yeah," Karim said. "Mort's says petrification wears off in a few weeks. But if that happened to me it might as well be permanent. My dad would just ground me forever as soon as I thawed." He could hear his dad's yelling in his head now.

"Let's get going," Spike said, annoyed.

Karim was just about to pull away from her and head for the exit when another image popped into his head.

A basilisk. A real live basilisk. Mortimer's put it at a Level 2 threat—not lethal. After years of Adventure Camp, of watching his father's old documentaries, of dreaming about seeing real monsters . . . In the image in his head, the basilisk stuck its forked tongue out at him, as if daring him. Why did his own imagination have to talk back to him?

He let Spike and Tommy lead the way, but Karim followed behind them as they ventured out from behind the staircase. He pulled out the mirrored goggles that he'd swiped from his dad's old adventuring gear box in the basement. He should at least *try* to take a look at the basilisk. Once they'd seen the creature, maybe they could all be satisfied and get out of there.

"This is so sweet!" Tommy said. "A real basilisk here in the school! Who would've thought?"

"No kidding. I've been seeing the adventure streamers talking about this," Spike said. "There are way more confirmed monsters popping up this season, some far outside their natural habitats too. No one knows why."

As they made their way through the school, Spike and Tommy were very carefully looking at the ceiling, using only their peripheral vision to guide them.

Karim caught sight of what he thought was the basilisk crawling along the ceiling tiles, but he tried to put it out of his mind. According to Mortimer's, basilisks liked caves and warm places, not climbing high into the ceiling.

They had walked only partway down the second grade hallway when Tommy called out, "Another one!" He was pointing at a freshly created stone statue at the end of the hall.

Karim had already snapped the goggles on, but it took him a little longer than the others to see the statue.

"It's the monster control guy!" Spike said, giggling. "They are all so incompetent."

As he got closer, Karim could see the man decked out in monster gear. He was in full armor, though it probably wasn't magical. Magical weapons were rare, but magical armor was almost unheard of. Only the most famous adventurers in the world had magical armor.

The guy did have mirrored goggles on just like Karim, but it looked like he had been pulling them up for a quick peek. As a result, this guy's entire body was turned to stone, along with his clothes and the goggles. His containment box was just sitting on the floor next to him.

"Had the gear, didn't use it properly. Typical," Spike said.

"Uh, typical of what?" Tommy asked.

Spike shrugged. "I dunno. People who aren't as awesome as me?" She sighed. "Karim, you're not going to do anything dumb like that, right?"

"Not after seeing that." Karim had to admit that his head was starting to swim from the odd angles of the world that the mirrored goggles presented him. "Also, I wonder what makes some things that are touching you turn to stone and others not."

"Maybe wonder that sort of thing after we catch it, huh?" Spike said. "Or if you meet one of the three known wizards in North America, you can ask them."

"Okay, so then where is it?" Tommy asked.

Karim looked around the hallway, trying to take it in the way that a basilisk would. The fun-house effect of his goggles definitely helped him feel like it was an alien environment. So many classrooms, all basically the same . . . For just a second he imagined himself as that scaly little devil, hunting for a safe place in a land full of two-legged giants. Where would he run?

"Basilisks like warm places," Karim said. "It came this way in order to get to Mr. Reynolds's room." The answer was out before he could consider whether he actually wanted to give his two insane friends the information that would take them all deeper into danger.

"Yeah," Tommy agreed. "Mr. Reynolds is like a billion years old and cranks the heat way up."

"Then what are we waiting for?" Spike was already starting down the hall, with Tommy at her heels.

Because if there was one thing Spike and Tommy liked, it was pulling Karim into more trouble. He sighed and jogged along after them. What if he didn't have the guts to handle this? He'd just have to hope he could invent some sort of strategy when the time came.

CHAPTER 4

TOMMY

It was go time. It was game on.

"Good luck," Karim said, knees practically knocking together from fright, as he handed Tommy the goggles. Without the mirrored lenses shielding Karim's face, Tommy could see the fear in his friend's eyes.

"So, find out where the basilisk is," Spike ordered, "and then we can come in without looking directly at it."

Tommy had known all along this would fall to him. Sometimes a job called for brawn and bravery. This was his moment.

"Three . . . two . . . one," he counted down. "Let's do this."

Tommy stepped into the room, and Spike slammed the door shut behind him. At the sound of the door slamming, something darted out in front of him and streaked across the room. Tommy immediately squealed and jumped up onto a desk. He really hoped his friends hadn't heard that, but he knew they had.

Tommy stepped down onto the floor. "I've spotted it," he said, trying to stay calm and confident. "It ran toward the front of the room. I'm onto the little sucker."

He advanced slowly, then leaned down close to the floor. Sometimes, to catch a monster, you had to sink to its level. That was what Tommy figured, anyway. The closest they'd ever come to hunting monsters was when they practiced capturing chickens and rabbits at Adventure Camp. The counselors said they weren't allowed to practice with real monsters because of "insurance reasons," which Tommy knew was just another way of saying, "We can't do it because we're total wimps and also hate fun."

There wasn't much light, but he could see something underneath Mr. Reynolds's desk. Right next to an old pair of dentures, he could see the outline of a lizard. Tommy pulled out his phone and used the flashlight to get a better look. The four-legged beast was about a foot long and covered in scales, with sharp ridges down its back and a crest on its head. A real live basilisk!

Tommy glanced at the door. Still closed. No way for his friends to see and make fun of him. He held his phone out, turned on the flashlight, fiddled until both he and the creature were in the frame, and snapped a quick selfie. He made sure to get the Brotein ("Drink our shakes. Push mad plates.") logo on his T-shirt in the shot, of course. The basilisk rustled a bit, but even with the flash, the creature didn't run for it.

Tommy checked the pic and grinned. Boom. Nailed it.

"Okay, guys, come in!" Tommy called. "It's hiding under the teacher's desk and doesn't look like it's gonna be coming out anytime soon."

Spike and Karim opened the door and entered the room, both carefully looking at the ceiling, occasionally bumping into chairs and desks as they made their way to the front of the room.

CHAPTER 5

SPIKE

The classroom was quiet except for the basilisk scratching under the desk and the hum of fluorescent lights above. The sound of sirens and teachers doing roll calls drifted in through a cracked window.

"The counselors at Adventure Camp would say we're making a big mistake," Karim warned, his eyes fixed on a point on the ceiling directly above them.

"You don't get to be a famous adventurer without taking a few chances." Tommy dropped and did a couple of push-ups. Even though Spike was looking at the ceiling, she rolled her eyes. Whatever Tommy needed to do to get psyched up, she supposed.

"We've got the right gear, the right plan, and the monster's one weakness," she said. "Hand me the weasel fur and we're good to go." This would be the first time they'd gotten an up-close look at a monster that Mort's ranked as Level 2. Spike was more than confident they could handle a challenge like this. The Level 1 monsters at Adventure Camp had been barely any danger at all.

"This. Will. Be. *Awesome*," Tommy said, pulling out a pouch of fur and opening it for easy access. Spike nodded. She had been skeptical when Tommy said he could get the fur, but the big lug had pulled through.

"Okay. Okay, no problem." Karim brushed his black hair from his face with a nervous flick. "My dad took out a whole nest of basilisks once, all by himself. *Without* weasel fur."

Under the desk, the basilisk hissed, as if taunting them to come closer. *Well*, Spike thought, *it's going to get exactly what it wants.*

"Here," Tommy said, handing Spike the goggles.

"Doesn't one of you want to do it?" she asked. "Those look a little big for me."

Karim shook his head. "This was *your* idea," he said, backing away with a scared look on his face. Karim was clever, but Spike wasn't sure he had the stomach for adventuring.

Spike looked over at Tommy.

"I found it," Tommy said. "And I got the weasel fur. But I don't think I can fit my arms there to make the grab. I'll be the backup, in case you need brute force, you know?"

"Cowards." Spike took the goggles from Tommy and pulled the strap around her head as tight as it would go. It looked like she would have to do the hard part. Again.

"Be careful," Karim warned her. "If you get so much as a scratch on these goggles, my dad will kill me."

"The basilisk's going to be paralyzed by the weasel fur," Spike said, rolling her eyes at the boys for what felt like the hundredth time that day. "It won't be able to move. Then we just take it out and we can get a closer look. It's shedding scales, so we can probably even get a few for souvenirs. Super easy."

Karim still looked uncertain, but Spike shrugged. They'd come this far; she wasn't going to turn back now. She looked around through the mirrored goggles, inspecting the slightly distorted view of the classroom.

"Okay, one of you stand in front of the desk, and the other behind it," she instructed. "To make the basilisk think it's trapped. I'll watch it and tell Tommy where to drop the fur."

They surrounded the desk as Spike crouched down. There was the basilisk, right up against the wall, just like Tommy said. Its tongue slipped in and out as it stared at her. Was it wondering why she wasn't turned to stone?

"Okay, Tommy," she said, raising her hand and indicating the spot along the top of the desk directly above the basilisk. "Drop the fur down there."

Long seconds passed as Tommy fumbled with the bag. Not surprisingly, he clearly hadn't practiced beforehand. Working with amateurs like this was always such a chore. Sure, this was Spike's first monster hunt too, but she had been preparing for it her whole life.

Finally, Tommy dropped the fur. From below, Spike watched as it drifted down through the small gap between the wall and the desk, and settled on and around the lizard.

The basilisk twitched once, then stopped moving.

"It shouldn't take long," Karim said, his low tone filled with awe. "Mort's says basilisks are frightened by even the *sight* of weasel fur."

Spike counted to twenty quietly. The basilisk stared at her for the entire time, perfectly still; the only movement was its nostrils flaring slightly.

"Okay, it must be paralyzed," she said.

"What do we do now?" Tommy asked. "Should I charge it? Is it time to try brute force?" He flexed an arm. Spike noted that while Tommy's arm *was* rather large, it wasn't particularly muscle shaped.

"Nope," Spike answered. "Now it's paralyzed for several hours. We just need to grab it."

Spike extended her arm ever so slowly, twisting slightly to get closer so that her arm could fit in the narrow space between the desk and the wall.

"I've got you now," she whispered as she reached out. Looking at the spiky ridges that ran down the basilisk's spine, she was very grateful that it was completely immobilized.

She was only a few inches away. And then she opened her hand and grasped . . .

Nothing.

By the time Spike's hand closed, the basilisk had darted out from under the desk, first toward Karim, who was jumping back in terror and holding his hands over his eyes. Then it came back straight at her.

Spike yelped, dodged sideways, tripped over a desk, and

went sprawling. As she fell, the goggles flew off her head and hit the wall with a sickening crunch.

"The goggles!" Tommy yelled. He picked them up and held the shattered frames.

Karim made a choked sound, like a dog that had its tail stepped on.

"Tommy!" Spike called. "Where did you get that weasel fur?!" The plan was perfect. Tommy must have messed it up somehow. Like usual.

"I just used my dad's beard trimmer on my sister's pet weasel, duh!" He backed away from the hissing basilisk, knocking over several chairs and a desk in the process.

"Um. Tommy. Your sister has a ferret," Karim pointed out. His eyes were glued shut, and he was steadily sliding along the wall, moving away from the basilisk.

"What? I thought weasels and ferrets were the same thing!" Tommy protested. "Like horses and ponies. Or . . . Wait, is the ferret the female and the weasel is the male?"

Karim groaned. "No, Tommy. They're not the same thing at all. Different species. Only weasel fur works."

"Seriously, Tommy?" Spike rolled her eyes. She tried to keep her attention on the basilisk, without looking directly at it, as the creature scampered around in a panic. Then, in a blur, it darted to the other side of the room and leaped into the air. Spike never could have imagined such a small lizard making a jump like that, but the basilisk somehow caught the bottom of the windowsill, pulled itself up, and wriggled through the crack in the window.

"Ugh," Karim said. "We never should have used my dad's goggles. He's going to end me."

"Hmm, maybe we should've gone with brute strength," Tommy said.

"Maybe *you* should've known the difference between a weasel and a ferret!" Spike shot back.

"Maybe we should've closed the window," Karim noted.

"Maybe we should get out of here," Spike suggested.

On that, they could all agree.

The basilisk escaped into the school's courtyard, which was totally enclosed. But when the trio got there, it was gone.

Honestly, to Karim that was a huge relief. Maybe they could just forget this whole ordeal and join the other students without anyone noticing.

"Where are you?" Tommy demanded, stalking around the courtyard like an angry mountain troll.

"We have to think systematically," Spike said. "What are all the places it could have gone?"

While Spike and Tommy examined each window and door, Karim took a deep breath. There were just too many options—four open windows, two doors—and there was always the chance that the creature could have climbed the walls. All Karim had to do was wait a minute for Spike to realize that this was hopeless.

But his mind was working overtime. What did basilisks

like? What did they hate? According to Mort's, basilisks hated open spaces, and they liked heat.

Karim tried to keep his eyes still, but instead his gaze darted from place to place, envisioning the courtyard the way a six-inch-tall lizard would see it. The doors and windows in this courtyard all led back to classrooms, none of them as warm as Mr. Reynolds's room had been.

"Shut up," Karim muttered to himself, but his imagination started offering up possibilities. Where else in the school would the basilisk want to go?

The basilisk was stuck in the school. It had been chased around by what were, to a basilisk, giants. First monster control, then three kids who showered it with fur. The poor lizard was trapped in this maze of classrooms—a world designed for creatures ten times its size.

Dark. Warm.

Karim's eyes caught a small grate at the base of the far wall. That would lead down. Down to the basement. Down to the boiler room, the warmest place in the school. But it was too small for the basilisk to fit through. Wasn't it? Maybe if it could squeeze through a crack in a window . . .

Karim tried to stop his legs, but they took him to the grate. He leaned down to inspect it. Two pieces of the metal grating were bent to the sides, one still gleaming with a fresh scratch. The image was perfectly clear in Karim's mind. That must have been where the basilisk's ridge cut as it pushed its way through.

"Find something?" Spike asked.

Karim blinked at Spike. Well, there went his plan to give up and go outside to safety. "It went through here, into the basement," he explained, pointing at the grate. "I imagine it's heading for the boiler room."

"Okay, let's get him," Tommy said. "Lizard bro is going *down*." He cracked his knuckles to underscore the point.

"Is this right?" Karim asked. "Should we maybe leave the basilisk alone?" He was still a little scared of the lizard with the petrifying glare, but Karim could sympathize with a creature that was looking for a place to hide.

Spike rolled her eyes. "Are you serious? The guy from monster control got turned to stone. If we don't catch the basilisk, monster control guy's buddies will probably come and use poison or something. We have to capture it or it will die."

Karim had to admit that Spike had a good point there.

"Come on, your dad would have this thing captured and delivered home by now!" Tommy said. "It's in your blood."

"I know, I know, he's the greatest," Karim said, waving the comment off. "But you're right. If we don't do something, the basilisk will keep turning people to stone, or monster control will probably kill it."

"It's settled, then." Spike led them to the nearest stairs.

"Yep, lizard bro is gonna get destroyed," Tommy said.

"I think you mean *captured for its own protection*," Karim corrected.

"Whatever." Tommy shrugged. "Same difference."

CHAPTER 7

TOMMY

Finally! They were going to catch a monster!

The basement was as dark as any dungeon or crypt Tommy could imagine. He thought it was just like an adventure straight from the classic adventure shows, like the one Karim's dad used to host back in the day.

"Ouch," Karim said as they entered the boiler room.

Tommy winced. The janitor was frozen in stone, his face a look of shock. One of his stone fingers was still up his nose.

"Well, I guess we were right," Spike said matter-of-factly. "And I guess Custodian Saunders here didn't get much warning..." She knocked on the janitor's head as though looking to see if anyone were home.

Tommy shook his head. Custodian Saunders had always been nice to them when he saw the three friends sneaking around on awesome adventures. He'd never ratted them out, not once. Poor guy. This rumor would probably get out for sure, even though everybody picked their nose, as far as

Tommy knew. You were just supposed to pretend you didn't. Like peeing in the pool.

"Hold still," Karim instructed, and they froze. The orange light from the boiler threw wild shadows on the walls.

After a long pause, a faint scratching sound came from behind a pile of boxes.

"It's dark in here," Karim said, grabbing an empty cardboard box from the pile. "If we could just get this box over the basilisk . . . But how are we going to see it?"

"If only we had weasel fur." Spike jabbed Tommy in the ribs.

"It's not *my* fault stretchy rodents come in two flavors!" Tommy complained. It really wasn't fair, having so many animals that looked the same. This was worse than that time in first grade when he'd followed some woman around the mall for half an hour, thinking it was his mom because they had the same coat.

"Whatever. Let's get this over with," Spike said. "Tommy and I will flush it out, and Karim can catch it under the box."

"Me?" Karim asked. "Are you sure—"

"You're the fastest," Spike interrupted. "Just do it. I'll tell you when."

Tommy and Spike loudly approached one side of the boxes while Karim crept up on the other, the box gripped in his hands.

"Here, little basilisk," Tommy said.

Spike stepped forward, stomping loudly.

Spooked, the basilisk shot the opposite direction, going straight for Karim. But instead of using the box, Karim jumped backward, squealing in terror. He tripped as the basilisk darted the other way, and ended up falling on his butt as the basilisk hid behind the boiler.

Spike and Tommy walked over to the boiler, but Karim simply sat there, staring after the basilisk.

"Really, Karim?" Spike complained.

"Sorry," Karim said, rubbing his butt. "I'll do it next time, I swear. I just . . . I was afraid I'd look at it if I tried to catch it."

"It was moving way too fast, anyway." Tommy stomped the floor in frustration. "How are we supposed to catch this thing if we can't even *look* at it?" Adventuring was supposed to be about heroically battling monsters and feats of strength, not chasing salamanders around the basement of his middle school.

"Just give me a minute," Spike said, brow furrowed in thought. Karim slumped down in a corner, hands pressed over his eyes.

"Whatever," Tommy said, pulling out his phone. "I'm going to see if I can get a shot of it for Instagram, at least." He leaned down and tried awkwardly to get both his face and a view of the boiler in the frame. It was important to get your face in the shot so people knew you were really there.

"Tommy!" Karim said. "That's it! You're a genius!"

"Huh?" Tommy answered. "I mean, I know I am. But . . . What did I do?"

CHAPTER 8

SPIKE

Karim jumped to his feet, phone in hand.

"Huh?" Tommy stared at him in confusion. "How is Instagram going to help us?"

Spike rolled her eyes and pulled out her phone. Was Tommy really that thick?

"The camera," she said, grinning. "We can see the basilisk *through* it." Karim's ideas might be a bit impractical at times, but Spike had to admit that he had nailed it.

A few seconds later they were all crouched around the boiler, peering at the screens of their smartphones. Spike could see the basilisk crouched in the dust behind it.

"Okay, let's try this one more time," she said. "Karim, you flush it out from the right side. Tommy, get ready with the box. I'll tell you when."

"Are we sure we should do this?" Karim held his phone at arm's length, and Spike could see that his hand was shaking. "Maybe we should just wait for the police to come?"

"We created this problem," Spike shot back. "We should be the ones to solve it."

Spike moved into position without giving Karim a chance to object. Karim found an old broom handle in a closet, then approached from the right side. Tommy grabbed the box and set up on the left. Spike crouched down so that she could see the basilisk under the boiler. She checked her phone. It had one missed call—from her dad. Shaking her head in disappointment, she dismissed the notification, then turned on the phone's flashlight. The lizard's spiky shape stood starkly at the back of the boiler.

"Okay, let's do this," Spike said.

Tommy looked through his own phone, holding it awkwardly while Karim prodded behind the boiler with the broom handle. Spike held her breath as she watched the broom handle get closer and closer to the basilisk. Finally, the basilisk bolted.

"Ready . . . NOW!" Spike said as the basilisk's dark silhouette reached Karim. Her body tensed as she realized that it might attack him. This really *was* dangerous. If Karim got hurt, his dad would find out about all this. And that could easily lead to all three of them getting pulled out of Adventure Camp this summer.

The box fell on the basilisk, but its tail was still sticking out through the corner, swishing wildly.

"Got you!" Tommy crowed, trying to hold the box as the creature struggled madly. Spike leaped to his aid and pushed the flailing tail under the box with her foot.

"Karim!" Spike gritted her teeth, holding on gamely. "Get over here!"

Karim jumped into action and helped them hold down the box. Suddenly, the box stopped shaking, though they could still hear the basilisk scratching inside.

"This cardboard won't hold for long," Karim said. "He's already poking a few holes in the side."

"Okay, just hold on!" Spike said, glancing around in a panic. She jumped up and quickly rummaged through the dim basement room.

She found a large and heavy trash bag in the corner. Spike slipped the bag over the cardboard box from one side, raising the box only a fraction of an inch so that the lizard couldn't escape.

"Let's go, it's clawing its way out!" Karim cried.

Through the clear plastic, Spike could see the basilisk poking its head through the box. "That thing can really chew! We need somewhere to put it—fast!"

"The freezer in the kitchen?" Tommy suggested.

"No, I've got it," Karim said. "The monster control guy's box was sitting next to him. It didn't get turned to stone!"

"Okay. Beast mode for real now!" Tommy said.

"Do it," Spike said. The lizard was thrashing about, and she doubted that she or Karim could hold on to it. She hated trusting someone else with this, but Tommy had hit his growth spurt. It had to be him. "Go!"

Tommy picked up the plastic garbage bag from the top,

held it closed, then ran for the stairs. Spike and Karim followed behind at a sprint.

The halls stood empty. The fluorescents were off and fire lights still flashed, giving the whole area a menacing and unfamiliar feel, like a spaceship after an alien attack.

"Faster!" Karim yelled. "It's breaking through!"

Spike could see it as well, the basilisk attacking the heavy clear plastic of the bag from the inside. The creature turned its head to her for a moment, but she glanced away just in time.

"Shake it!" Karim yelled.

Spike watched as Tommy shook the plastic bag while he ran, sending the basilisk tumbling around inside. The remains of the cardboard box were now a shredded mess.

They quickly reached the petrified monster control guy, who still had a small cage at his side. Karim held the opening of the trash bag against the cage's door. Spike took the other end of the bag, shaking it madly. The creature lost its grip and tumbled into the cage.

As the basilisk lay stunned in its confines, Karim pulled the bag away and slammed the cage door shut. The locking mechanism clicked into place automatically.

The three looked at one another, panting from the effort. Spike could feel sweat dripping as she pulled in ragged breaths. From inside the cage, the basilisk hissed and scratched, furious at being trapped.

"We'd better get out of here before someone sees us," Spike said.

"Don't worry," a woman's voice said behind them, and all three kids jumped. "Your secret's safe with us."

A man and a woman appeared behind them. Both were wearing black uniforms with a stylized A on the chest.

Tommy and Karim looked on in shock, but Spike wasn't so easily shaken. "Who are you?" she demanded.

"We're here to pick up this little pest," the man said, grabbing the cage. "Your friendly neighborhood monster control bureau failed, so they called in the *real* professionals."

"Not too shabby," the woman added, inspecting the cage. "We'll have to keep our eyes on you."

"What?" Tommy blurted out. "Who . . . are you?"

"Best get a move on," the man said, tapping his phone. "I just gave the all clear, and the school staff will be coming back in soon."

Spike knew when it was time to make a graceful exit. She turned and ran for it, Tommy and Karim close behind.

CHAPTER 9

TOMMY

"That . . . was . . . so . . . *cool!*" Tommy said between massive gulps of air.

Was this the greatest moment of his life? He paused for a second. He still felt awesome. Maybe even more awesome than before. Was *this* the greatest moment of his life?

Karim was staring blankly, silently shaking his head back and forth. He didn't seem excited, just more scared than ever.

"You okay?" Tommy asked. Karim probably needed to do more bicep curls or something. That would get his confidence up.

"Uh, yeah, sure," Karim said. "It's just . . . That was crazy. My dad's going to kill me. If we get caught—*when* we get caught."

"We'd better find a way out of here," Spike said.

"We can sneak out through the lower parking lot," Karim suggested. "If we don't get there soon, we'll be in huge trouble."

Spike drew a deep breath, and the trio went into the hallway. A moment later they were slipping out the back door. The other two had an easy time slinking behind car to car, but Tommy wasn't a frail little thing like them. He had to run hunched over. Sneaking was absolutely the worst.

They looped all the way around through the parking lot, eventually rejoining the crowd from behind. Tommy was breathing heavily, but everyone's attention was on the school, where the two monster hunters in dark sunglasses and smart black uniforms were strutting out of the building, holding the basilisk in its carrier as though they'd been the ones to capture it.

"There you are," a voice said from behind them, dripping with hostility. "What excuse do you have *this* time?"

CHAPTER 10

SPIKE

The three spun around. Sally "the Sheriff" Smithfield stood there, glowering at them from behind her thick-rimmed glasses.

Spike's stomach clenched. Their school's guidance counselor, aka the Sheriff, had been trying to throw the trio in detention ever since they got caught putting an acidic toad in Donna Ford's backpack. "She said I had a boy's haircut" hadn't been a good enough justification, apparently. Spike still thought it was a reasonable response. Being smart and tough didn't make her some kind of smelly boy. Ugh.

"I don't know what you're talking about," Karim bluffed, but his voice quavered slightly. Spike really needed to give him some lessons in lying with conviction.

"Can I ride in the fire truck?" Tommy asked in an innocent voice. "I wanna ride in the fire truck!"

Spike grimaced. Tommy had long ago learned that if he acted like an idiot, he wouldn't get in trouble. Somehow Spike knew she couldn't get away with the same trick. She'd mouthed off one too many times for that.

"Why is it I've only just seen the three of you, when everyone else has been here for over half an hour?" the Sheriff demanded. "Well, Colleen?"

"Don't. Call. Me. That," Spike shot back through gritted teeth, glaring at the Sheriff. "The name is *Spike*."

The Sheriff glared right back. "Whatever made-up name you want to call yourself, Colleen," she said with a sigh. "Several students have been turned to stone. It'll be a long, long detention if I find out you're involved."

Spike stared her down silently. She knew better than to talk back to authority figures. Even if you were innocent, they'd figure out a way to twist what you said and get you in trouble. It was even worse when you were totally guilty.

"And don't you two get poor Tommy mixed up in any of your trouble," the Sheriff said.

"We wouldn't dream of it," Karim answered. "Tommy is a perfect little angel."

Spike couldn't help but add, "Yes, he's an adorable, rosy-cheeked little baby cupid."

Tommy shot her a furious glance, but his expression was back to normal when Sally turned to look at him.

"Can the firefighters spray me with a hose?" Tommy asked. "It's hot out here!"

"I'm watching you," the Sheriff said, eyeing Spike and Karim. "So watch yourselves."

A few days later, Karim was growing more and more convinced that his friends were insane. That was the only explanation for it. Some wiring in their heads had gotten fused from watching too many live adventure streams, and Tommy and Spike had lost their senses of self-preservation.

That explained them, anyway. The only thing that Karim couldn't explain was why he kept going along with their shenanigans. Though he had to admit, watching a professional adventure streamer like Mad Mackenzie did make it seem fun.

"I still can't believe the Sheriff didn't nab us," Karim said as he flicked through the streams on Tommy's iPad and pulled up Mad Mackenzie's. The video opened with Mad Mackenzie in her garage, showing off her latest gear.

"It's a good thing school guidance counselors aren't allowed to dust for fingerprints or administer truth serum,"

Spike said as they watched Mad Mackenzie explain how to sharpen a magical dagger properly.

"We're going to have to be more careful at school," Karim said. "The Sheriff will be watching us, and if my dad thinks I'm playing around with monsters . . ." He didn't need to say what would happen. Spike and Tommy had heard plenty about Mr. Khalil's stance on adventuring.

Tommy was on a weight bench on the other side of the garage, and Karim could hear him grunting as he bench-pressed weights into the air. Karim and Spike said they would work out with Tommy in his family's garage, but like usual they ended up getting bored and watching adventure streamers.

"If you're out there adventuring this season, be careful," Mad Mackenzie warned on-screen. "This is the craziest one we've had in a long time—monsters are turning up in places they don't belong, outside their usual habitats. Could it be some sort of environmental issue? Or does something else have them riled up? In any event, be prepared. Like I always say, keep your weapons sharp and your wits sharper. Until next time."

The weights slammed as Tommy returned the barbell to the rack.

"What is it, Elissa?" Tommy grumbled loudly. "We can tell you're there. Can't you see I'm hanging out with my friends?"

Karim and Spike both turned to see Tommy's younger sister standing in the doorway, silhouetted by the lights from the kitchen.

Usually Karim would be right there with Tommy, annoyed

that Elissa was spying on them. But as Elissa stepped into the light, Karim could see that her cheeks were stained with tears. She gave a sad sniffle.

"Are you okay?" Karim asked. "What's wrong?"

Tommy's sister had been known to throw a tantrum now and then, but he'd never seen her like this. She looked really upset.

Tommy could see it too. "I'm sorry, Lissa," he said, standing up. "What's wrong?"

She ran down and grabbed her big brother in a tight hug. Also unusual. As far as Karim knew, Elissa and Tommy were more the squabbling type of siblings than the hugging type.

Karim and Spike stood frozen for a long moment as Elissa sobbed.

"Mom lost the case, Tom-Tom," Elissa said between heaving breaths.

"It's okay." Tommy looked down at his sister in confusion. "She'll have other cases. She'll be sad for a few days, but then she'll be home more than she has been lately. That will be nice, right?"

Karim felt bad, but he had to admit he was a bit conflicted. Mrs. Wainwright had been representing a bank robber suing a bank. The robber slipped on the marble floor and threw out his back while trying to escape with a magical artifact he'd stolen from one of the safe deposit boxes.

"Mom's lost cases before. Money might be a little tight for a while, but don't worry. We'll be fine. Christmas isn't for a while, anyway!"

"But . . . but . . . Adventure Camp!" Elissa could barely get the words out. "Dad said that since Mom didn't win the case, they can't afford to send us to Adventure Camp this year."

Tommy's face fell. Karim and Spike looked at each other. For the past four years they'd gone to Adventure Camp together. They had spent every summer learning knots, climbing, swordsmanship, monster tracking, and mystical botany.

Tommy turned to his friends as his sister continued to sob. "I've been plenty of times; it's no huge deal if I can't go this year. But I've been telling her about it for ages now. This was supposed to be her first year."

Karim's dad despised the whole thing, but even so, it had been Karim's favorite time of every year since they started. He remembered being an eight-year-old like Elissa, so excited to go for his first time and learn adventuring skills. He was so excited—but also scared—that he didn't sleep for two days beforehand. As a result, he ended up panicking on the ropes course. He had to be tied to one of the counselors and then lowered from a tree. Now Adventure Camp seemed safe and fun, but the idea of real adventuring still made him want to hide in his room.

The three escorted Elissa back into the house, doing their best to comfort her. Eventually, she calmed down enough to give her brother a final hug, then trudged upstairs to finish her homework.

"I wish I could help," Spike said. "But Luis takes all my money from selling OrgoLocoLemonade and puts it into my college fund." Luis was Spike's dad, but for some reason she always called him Luis. Karim figured it had something to do with him divorcing her mother and moving across the country. He couldn't imagine how hard that must be.

Karim shook his head. He was still amazed that Spike was able to start a successful lemonade brand by making up fake, dangerous ingredients and promising that they weren't in it. Karim had been astounded by how much people would pay for "tachyon-free" and "certified zero theta radiation" drinks.

Tommy sighed. "This is why we need to be adventurers for real. Adventurers usually come with sweet loot at the end, right?"

"That's kind of the point, isn't it?" Spike said. "That and proving that we can take it on. I'm tired of people telling us what we can't do."

"What about because it helps people?" Karim ventured.

"Yeah, sure, that too," Spike said.

"Right. I guess so," Tommy added.

That's when the doorbell rang.

CHAPTER 12

TOMMY

"Tommy! Get the door," a deep voice roared from the living room. "They're in the middle of the rose ceremony, and I have to make sure Sophia chooses right!" The bellowing was Tommy's dad, better known as Big Tom.

Tommy shook his head. His dad's obsession with his dating shows was ridiculous, but at least it meant Dad was distracted. The few times when Dad tried to have "fun father-son time" had been even worse. Wearing tight shoes at the stinky bowling alley was not Tommy's idea of fun.

Spike tiptoed up to the door and peered through the peephole. "He's got a weapon!" she whispered.

Tommy leaned in and took a look for himself. A scrawny young man was standing outside, holding a rusty battle axe. By the time he stepped back, Spike had found Big Tom's welding mask. She was holding it in a two-handed grip, ready to use it as a club.

"We shouldn't open it," Karim said. "Should we call the cops or something?"

"He may be older than us, but he's a scrawny pipsqueak. I could totally take him." Tommy gripped the doorknob, and Spike gulped as he opened the door.

The boy stared at them for a long second, eyes wide. Tommy couldn't see the boy's knees through his baggy pants, but from the rest of his posture it looked like they would be knocking together. Tommy straightened up a bit, knowing that he cut a pretty imposing figure.

"Hello, ma'am and sirs," the boy said, his voice squeaking. "I'm Jason, an AppVenture Independent Contractor. I—I'm, uh, here to help with your monster problem. They said it was, um, a gremlin?"

"Dad, did we call someone about gremlins?" Tommy shouted back into the house. "Do we have gremlins? Because that would be awesome."

"No!" Big Tom wailed from the living room. "Tell them to go away! I'm busy with my show, and she just sent Brent home! But their last date was *soooooo* romantic!"

Tommy shrugged and turned back to the skinny young man on the doorstep. "I don't think we have any gremlin issues. Someone must have given you wrong information."

"Uh . . . is this 621 Waldorf Ave?"

Tommy shook his head. "This is 619. You want Mrs. Peabody next door." He pointed to his neighbor's house. This pipsqueak was a mess.

"Oh, okay. Sorry to bother you, sir," the young man said, letting his rusty axe hang down at his side.

Tommy closed the door and shook his head. "If that

scrawny dude can go monster hunting, why not us? I could trash him blindfolded."

"I hope that axe has some serious enchantment," Spike said. "Gremlins aren't big, but they can be vicious little things."

"But they're tiny!" Tommy protested. "How could something so small be that big a deal?" It was ridiculous. He guessed he could crush a gremlin with one hand.

"My cousins had gremlins in their basement once," Spike told them. "They tried everything, but gremlins are just so fast and clever. Eventually, they had to carpet bomb the place with itching powder in order to get them to leave. The basement was basically unusable for a year, but they said it was worth it to have the gremlins out of the house."

A loud squeal erupted from outside. They crowded up to the bay windows to look at the house next door.

"Owie! It bit my bum!" the scrawny young man yelled as he scampered away from Mrs. Peabody's house. He retreated down the road, grasping his battle axe to his chest like a security blanket.

"Amateur," Karim said with disdain.

"My cousins said they can bite like nothing else," Spike said. "It leaves welts for weeks."

Tommy glanced down at his phone and started hopping up and down. "Oh, oh! Mad Mackenzie is about to start live streaming! She's going to ride a spike-horned ironhoof!"

A few minutes later Tommy grabbed his tablet and a Brotein ("Be the bro you want to see in the world") bar, and the three were clustered around as it loaded up Mad Mackenzie's channel.

"Ugh, more ads," Karim groaned. "Can't we just watch the recap videos from her adventure yesterday?"

"Already saw them. Nightmare bats. Pretty good stuff," Spike said.

Tommy nodded. He'd seen those videos too. The way she cleared out the nest of nightmare bats with a supercharged leaf blower and an enchanted trident had been impressive. Mad Mackenzie was definitely the best adventure streamer on the net.

Another ad started. A gong rang and an annoyingly handsome man wearing a hoodie over a business suit popped onto the screen. The gong rang again.

"Hi, I'm Mike Tuckerville," the man started. "I created AppVenture in order to connect adventurers with adventures. Need an imp dispelled? A manticore chased from your woods?" The man flashed a toothy grin. "Just download our app to your smartphone and call up one of our Independent Adventure Contractors today. Let AppVenture solve your monster problem tonight!"

"AppVenture. Isn't that what that guy at the door said he was from?" Spike had been wondering who would send out such an inexperienced adventurer. The big professional adventure firms, like Monster Hunters, Inc., usually sent teams of four with tons of gear and a couple decades of experience among them.

"Yup, that was it," Karim answered. "And the people who picked up the basilisk were wearing that logo on their uniforms."

The man's face disappeared and a very fast-talking voice started, *"Independent Adventure Contractors are not insured, licensed, indemnified, or protected in any way by AppVenture. Results may vary. Hire them at your own risk."*

Suddenly, Mike Tuckerville, perfectly smarmy in his hoodie and tie, returned. "So let us handle the adventuring—and consider your monster problems solved!"

"That Tuckerville guy seems like a total butt," Karim said after the ad was over.

"But I bet he's making tons of money, with the surge in monster incidents this season," Spike said.

"Yeah, probably," Karim answered. "Remember when adventurers used to be cool?"

"Sure," Spike said. "But these guys are getting both the glory and the money these days."

"And those black uniforms did look pretty sweet!" Tommy added.

"Maybe," Karim said. "I guess there's no measuring up to my dad, anyway."

"I mean, the Fang was the greatest," Tommy said. He knew it was tough for Karim, knowing that his dad had been one of the biggest adventurers of all time. "But even he started out somewhere, right?"

"Sure, I guess," Karim said with a shrug.

Spike watched Tommy stroke the six hairs on his chin thoughtfully. The hairs were certainly not anywhere near enough to be a beard—which Tommy insisted it was—but Spike did wonder how many more would need to sprout before she could no longer deny that it was a beard. Tommy might get there eventually, but Spike had a couple more years at least to keep making fun of him.

"Mrs. Peabody still hasn't gotten rid of that gremlin," Tommy said. "I saw that kid Jason again last night. He spent half an hour walking up and down the street getting psyched up. And then three minutes after he went inside, he came running out, yelling something about the gremlin biting his nose."

"Sounds like a nasty little thing," Karim said. "Poor kid."

The school day was over and the three friends were waiting for the buses to arrive. Other students bustled around them, chatting about sports or celebrities or video games.

Spike was glad that she and her friends had real, serious monster things to discuss. There were two things in the world Spike hated the most: small talk and people who called her Colleen. Also broccoli, but everyone hated that.

Spike's phone buzzed, and *Luis Hernandez* flashed on the screen. Her dad. Again. At least she'd changed the contact so that it didn't say *Dad* anymore. She pressed the red decline button. He wasn't going to ruin another day. Spike took a deep breath and focused her mind back on the present.

"Gentlemen," Spike said, "it sounds to me like another opportunity has appeared. There's another monster running around, and someone has to handle it."

Karim gulped. "It sounds like that kid Jason had a really tough time in there . . ."

Spike shrugged. "I didn't say that it would be easy!"

"But we do need . . ." Tommy started, then took a long swig from his Brotein ("Might may not make right, but it sure feels right") shake as he thought. "We do need a magical sword. You can't fight monsters without a magical sword."

Spike nodded. "That's certainly true enough. Most monsters are immune to normal weapons. We would need something enchanted."

After a moment, Spike and Tommy both looked expectantly at Karim.

"What?" Karim's eyes widened. "WHAT?! You think I'm going to—"

"Where else could we possibly get a magical weapon? And it's a good one," Spike said.

"My dad would *kill* me!" Karim protested. "He keeps it in a display case in his study! He would see if it was missing! I'm lucky he never checks his gear box in the basement or he would notice his mirrored goggles are missing."

Spike figured Karim would have that reaction. The kid was practically scared of the sound of his own footsteps.

"Tommy?" Spike said, raising an eyebrow. She had already worked this bit out with him. When you needed to convince someone of something, you had to go in with a plan.

"Well"—Tommy looked down sheepishly—"before you moved to town, I used to be a . . . big fan . . . of your dad."

Spike wasn't a superfanboy like Tommy, but she got it. Karim's dad, Yousef "the Fang" Khalil, was world famous. Before his injury with a band of frost trolls in Calgary, he'd been one of the Adventure Channel's top stars.

"I used to binge-watch old episodes of his show every weekend," Tommy continued. "I was obsessed."

Spike remembered the first time she and Tommy had met Mr. Khalil, when he had driven the three of them to Adventure Camp. Spike had perfectly kept her cool, of course. But Tommy had turned red and let out a little squeal every time Mr. Khalil said something or glanced into the back seat.

"Yeah," Karim said wistfully. "Of course, that was before the Adventure Channel stopped showing real live adventurers and started showing fake stuff about UFOs and ghosts."

"Focus, boys!" Spike said.

"Oh, right." Tommy took another gulp of his Brotein ("There's a muscle-bound hulk with no neck inside all of us") shake. "For my eighth birthday, my parents got me a replica of Sidesplitter."

Sidesplitter was the sword that Mr. Khalil wielded for most of his adventures. Spike had always thought that the episode of *Adventure Incorporated* where the Fang won Sidesplitter from the lair of a manticore was one of the greatest of all time.

Spike grinned. "See, all you need to do is switch it with the replica. Your dad will never know the sword is gone."

Karim's black hair swished as he shook his head.

"Dad says that if I ever even *think* of adventuring, he'll ground me until I'm thirty." Karim looked at the ground.

"And there's his first mistake. That's a crazy, ridiculously harsh punishment," Spike reasoned.

"That's supposed to make me feel better?" Karim asked, putting a hand on his head.

"If he were serious," Spike explained, "the punishment would be realistic. He's exaggerating because he's just trying to scare you off. And Tommy needs this. If we don't get the money, he and his sister won't be able to go to Adventure Camp this summer."

Tommy nodded along.

"I want to go adventuring too," Karim said, "but not enough to steal Sidesplitter from my dad!"

"You won't do it? Not even for me?" Spike asked. It was time to push. Without the magical sword, they would be as ineffective as a declawed manticore.

"He'll end me. Like, literally."

Spike sighed, shaking her fists in exasperation. "Tommy, a little help here?"

"I'm not worried, bro," Tommy said, taking another swig. "Karim wants to be an adventurer. There's nothing in the world he wants more. He's gonna steal the sword."

"Okay, okay. I'll do it." Karim sat silently for a long minute. Finally, he sighed. "But we are *not* getting caught."

Karim crept across the dining room. His heartbeat felt like a hummingbird practically exploding in his chest. His mom was still at work for another hour, and his dad had gone into the office down the hall, where he was on a conference call with the producers of a movie he was consulting for. Karim had to wait two days in order to find the right moment to make the snatch.

"This scene doesn't make sense. A gremlin would never do that," Karim heard his dad say from the other room. "They always bite first and ask questions later."

Was Karim really going to do this? His dad always said the sword would be his one day. Still, Karim didn't like it, even if his friends were counting on him.

In one hand he held the replica Sidesplitter, while in the other was the key to the display case where the real sword was kept, which Karim had swiped from his dad's sock drawer.

"And in the next scene," his dad continued, "the adventurers leave their gear behind. Every experienced adventurer knows the first rule of adventuring is never leave your pack."

Karim took a deep breath. He closed his eyes as he slipped the key into the lock and turned it. The click of the lock sounded like a sonic boom in the quiet room. He expected his mom to walk in, or his dad to appear with accusing eyes.

But neither happened. He picked up the real Sidesplitter, forged from pure meteorium, and set the replica in its place. They were the same weight, balanced just the same. Tommy's dad had definitely gotten an expert fake.

Meanwhile, Karim's dad was patiently explaining to Hollywood producers how a dragon's flame sac needs time to reignite after use.

Karim quietly tiptoed up the stairs. No one yelled. No alarms went off. A minute later, he had returned the key to his dad's sock drawer and stowed the magical sword in a golf club bag.

When he was done, he yelled, "I'm heading over to Tommy's." Karim waited a long moment, holding his breath.

His dad came down the hall into the dining room, maneuvering his wheelchair into the front hall. Even though his signature long hair was cut short and many years had passed since his TV star days, Yousef "the Fang" Khalil still had an imposing look that made him a favorite for adventure talk shows and a frequent guest expert on the news.

"Going golfing?" his dad asked.

"Oh, um," Karim started, "Tommy just wants to borrow

my clubs." Which was actually true—Tommy wanted to hit apples into La Tuna Canyon to see how far they could go.

"Well, whatever you're up to, have fun," Karim's dad said. "I've got to go write up some notes from that call."

An hour later, Sidesplitter gleamed as Karim pulled the sword out of the golf club carrier.

Tommy, Spike, and Karim were all in Tommy's basement, where a large box of Mrs. Wainwright's old lawn gnomes was "accidentally" wedged against the door. That way no one could stumble in on them and see the sword.

"Sweet!" Tommy intoned as Karim hefted the sword. "It looks so sharp!"

Sidesplitter was three feet long, with a grip large enough for two hands, and a pommel encrusted with jewels and engraved with an elaborate red-and-gold pattern.

"Okay, I stole my dad's magical sword," Karim said. "If we lose this thing, it's the end of the world for me, so here are the ground rules." He tried his best to look serious. "One, it never goes out of my sight. Two, no one uses it but me." Karim had been thinking this over and over, and it just seemed more and more crazy every time. How had he let his friends talk him into this?

"Fine," Spike said with a sigh. "But there's just one issue we need to deal with first." She took the sword from Karim and examined it. "This is a famous sword. If anyone sees us with it, they'll start asking questions that we won't want to answer."

Karim nodded and his stomach sank. He hadn't thought

about that. BuzzFeed actually ranked Sidesplitter as number seventy-two in its "Great American Artifacts Power Ranking" listicle last year. Karim knew that those rankings were more based on reputation than actual power. And as his dad always said, it's whoever wields the sword who matters most. But the sword was recognizable enough that if anyone saw it, word would get out for sure.

"Luckily, I have a solution," Spike said as she pulled out a bottle of something and began brushing it onto the sword's jeweled pommel.

Karim leaned forward to look at the bottle. The words *Violet Sparkle Eminence* were written on the label, right above *long-lasting nail polish*.

"Oh. My. Gosh." Karim stared at Spike, slack jawed. "You're putting sparkly purple nail polish on one of the most powerful artifacts in the world!"

"Re*lax*," Spike assured. "We'll take it off when we're done. This is an epic enchanted blade. Not even something super corrosive like sour ooze could hurt it. Short of being dropped in a volcano, there's nothing that can harm this sword."

She finished up the hilt, then ran nail polish along the red etchings on the blade. Karim felt like vomiting but just stared in horror. But still, Spike had a point. If anyone saw this sword out and about, it would be all over the adventuring blogs instantly.

"Plus . . ." Spike said as she wiggled her toes in her flip-flops. "Now it matches my new pedicure!" Her toes glittered with Violet Sparkle Eminence—whatever that was supposed to be.

"Since when do you paint your toenails?" was all that Karim, still reeling, could think to ask. Spike never wore anything like jewelry or makeup, except for the ring on her right index finger. And she always said the ring had belonged to her grandma, so it didn't count.

"Yeah, I seem to remember you punching your aunt in the solar plexus when she tried to give you a 'miracle makeover' last Thanksgiving," Tommy added, slurping down the last of his Brotein ("Don't talk the talk—flex the flex") shake.

"Your solar plexuses are looking tempting right about now." Spike glared at both of them and cracked her knuckles. "And for your information, I had my mom help me this afternoon."

"Okay, okay," Tommy said, backing away.

Karim would have done the same. He knew the two essential rules of warfare: (1) Don't invade Russia in the wintertime and (2) don't provoke Spike when she's already cranky.

"What next?" he asked.

Spike grinned. "Tomorrow, we catch ourselves a gremlin."

This. Was. Going. To. Be. *Awesome!*

Tommy stepped forward and knocked on Mrs. Peabody's door, standing up as straight as he could. Good posture was, like, 50 percent of making a good first impression. The rest, of course, was being ridiculously jacked. Another couple of months in the Temple of Body Sculpting (conveniently located in his garage) and he was sure he'd get there.

"I guess that other guy didn't get the job done," Karim said.

Tommy noticed that Karim was carefully standing back a bit, letting Spike and Tommy stand closer to the door. That was fine by Tommy—he was a tank, and tanks stood in front.

"He's probably at home icing his butt," Spike added. "If either of you screw up and get me bit, you're going to pay."

It was no big surprise that the scrawny kid had failed. Monster hunting was serious business, and you needed serious brawn to get the job done.

The door opened, and a gray-haired woman with stooped shoulders opened the door.

"What do you want?" Mrs. Peabody demanded, glaring over the top of her bifocal glasses at them. "I'm in the middle of a game here."

"Your contractor, Jason from AppVenture, wasn't able to solve your monster problem, so we've been sent here to do the job properly," Spike said.

Tommy nodded. They hadn't exactly been sent by anyone, but it wasn't exactly a lie either. Spike had a "creative" relationship with the truth.

"You three?" Mrs. Peabody asked, raising an eyebrow. "That gremlin seemed pretty nasty!"

Tommy growled and stood up extra tall but didn't say any of the retorts that came to mind about her being the old lady who lived next door. They were being paid to help her, after all.

"We're very experienced and have a track record of monster hunting success," Spike said smoothly. "Can you tell us where the gremlin has been sighted?"

Mrs. Peabody shrugged. "Okay, well, it's your butts on the line. The dang thing has taken up residence in the attic. I think I saw it run up there just a few minutes ago. I can't get up there to get out my old game controllers. These fancy new ones just aren't any good."

Mrs. Peabody stepped back and the three friends trooped into the living room. There was a big-screen TV wider across than Tommy was tall, and it displayed a line of scores from a video game.

"You play *Martians vs. Marines*?" Tommy asked, jaw dropping. It was one of his favorite games, even if he wasn't all that good at it. It was the kind of game where all you needed to do was shoot stuff. He liked that.

"It looks like she doesn't just play," Spike said, pointing to the top of the score screen. Above everyone else, with the highest score, there was a single username. "PeaBodySlam. Is that you, Mrs. Peabody?"

Mrs. Peabody sat down on the couch, in a place that looked dented from years of holding her body in exactly that position. "I'm retired, my husband passed away, my kids and grandkids live on the East Coast, and I have osteoporosis like you wouldn't believe," she said. "What else should I do with my time?"

"It's just . . . not what I expected," Tommy admitted. He'd always thought of Mrs. Peabody as the old lady who took five minutes to walk down the driveway to her car.

Mrs. Peabody shrugged. "The money I win from tournaments helps pay the bills. Plus, I like crushing the life out of kids who say dirty things on the microphone. I always say that a head shot is the best comeback."

The three looked at one another, too surprised to say anything.

"Now go do your job and don't distract me. Having this gremlin causing trouble has really hurt my KDR. It keeps chewing through my cables just enough so they flake out randomly."

"KDR?" Karim whispered as they walked up the stairs to the second floor.

"Kill-to-Death Ratio," Spike explained. "It's how many players she takes out for each time they get her."

On the screen, Mrs. Peabody used a ray gun the size of a small tree to blast away a lizard alien on what looked like the Great Wall of China. Tommy loved the dedication to realism that the guys who made *Martians vs. Marines* had.

The three tromped up the stairs to the second floor. Everything was printed in floral patterns—the walls, the pillows, the chairs. It was a bit odd for a lady who was downstairs playing first-person shooters competitively. After a minute, they found the pull-down door to the attic, and Spike motioned for them all to be silent. A few seconds later, they heard a faint scratching from above them.

"That must be it," Tommy whispered, his heart twitching in his chest. "A real monster, right here on my block!" A real monster that they could punch!

"Right, so we need a plan," Spike said in a hushed voice. "What's our strategy here?"

"Can't we just smack it with the sword?" Tommy asked. That was his favorite type of adventuring. He got pretty bored of the stuff with clues, plans, sabotage, and all that.

Spike sighed, then turned to Karim. "What does Mortimer's Monsterpedia say?"

Karim quickly pulled up the entry on his phone so they could read it.

Tommy shook his head. Why did they need to do all this research? Why couldn't they just charge in and start hitting things?

GREMLIN

LEVEL 3 MONSTER

Gremlins are small, human-shaped creatures with wiry builds and blue skin. They typically stand about two feet tall.

HABITAT: Gremlins are thought to have originated in the British Isles but have spread around the world to most industrialized nations by stowing away on ships and, since the twentieth century, commercial aircraft. They delight in causing trouble, in particular by sabotaging technology.

THREAT ANALYSIS: Gremlins are Level 3 monsters not because they are strong, but because they are mischievous and spiteful. Their most obvious weapon is their painful bite, but the real danger is that they are fiercely intelligent and will trick you into jumping into a dangerous ravine without a twinge of guilt. They are immune to most conventional weapons and damage. In fact, there are reports of gremlins being hit by trucks or crushed by tank treads and surviving.

WEAKNESSES: Gremlins rely primarily on their incredibly sharp sight. Their eyes give them excellent peripheral vision. If you can get them in the darkness or otherwise restrict their eyesight, they will be at a major disadvantage. Only enchanted weapons can harm them, and thus they are extremely afraid of all magical items.

■ ■ ■

"It's probably too fast for that," Karim answered, shaking his head. "But they're really afraid of magical weapons."

"We can use that," Spike said.

"Yeah!" Karim said, lighting up. "We can chase it into a trap. Maybe a pit trap?"

"Okay, sure." Tommy shrugged. He was still annoyed that they couldn't just hit it with the sword. Shouldn't they at least *try* the simple approach?

"No," Spike said. "Too hard to get it to go to the right place. Also, that's a lot more digging than I feel like doing."

"Do gremlins have any weaknesses?" Tommy asked. Maybe it would have something they could use.

"Yeah, ferret fur," Spike said with a wicked grin. "Tommy, can you get some for us?"

"Watch it, you," Tommy said with a growl. He'd looked it up on the internet later. Ferrets and weasels looked *exactly* the same. That whole thing was not his fault.

"Not really," Karim said. "They're small, crazy fast, and have supersharp eyesight. They tend to wait until you get close, then blow by you and escape." Karim scrolled and kept reading. "Also, they can jump down pretty much any distance. Like ants."

"Okay," Spike said. "Let's think methodically. Is there

anything there we can use? Maybe the fact that it's possible to get close to them before they run?"

"Yeah!" Karim said.

Tommy sat back and took out a Brotein ("'My muscles are too big' . . . said no one ever") bar to munch on. Best to let Karim and Spike handle this sort of thing. They'd let him know what his job was once they hatched a plan. He focused on tightening his core up with some quick flexing.

"We'll use its own advantages against it," Karim was saying when Tommy tuned back in to the conversation a few minutes later.

"Okay, I like it. Now that we've cased out the joint and have a plan," Spike said, "we're going to need some gear. Tommy, you stay here and guard the attic door. Don't let it come down."

She pointed at the edge of the stairs. The pull-down stairs, even raised, weren't quite the right size for the space they were in, and there was a gap of several inches between the bottom stair and the frame. "That's probably how it comes in," she said.

Tommy gingerly sat down on one of the plush chairs with a nice paisley print, putting some of the pillows onto the floor, out of his way.

"Taste my grenades!" they heard Mrs. Peabody yell from below.

"We're going to need something to hold the gremlin in," Spike said as she and Karim went back down the stairs.

"And some sort of protection for Tommy. These little things can be pretty aggressive."

"And I have an idea for how we can neutralize its eyesight," Karim said before their voices faded away.

Tommy settled into the chair, unwrapping the rest of his snack. Sit here and look intimidating? That was a job Tommy could handle.

A few minutes later, their plan was ready for action. It wasn't the simplest strategy, but it had two different ways they could win, so she liked that part about it.

Spike stood outside Mrs. Peabody's house, phone in hand. "You ready?"

"Good to go," Tommy said on the other end. "Do you really think this pot will hold him?"

"It's stainless steel!" Spike said. "Just stuff him in there." She had looted the pot from her mom's kitchen. Ms. Hernandez only used it on days when they had a bunch of guests over, anyway.

Tommy was getting a chance to try it his way first. Spike didn't expect him to succeed, but she hadn't bothered to tell him that. Besides, maybe he'd get incredibly lucky and charging straight after the gremlin would work perfectly.

"We're climbing up the stairs now," Karim's voice came

through the phone. "I've got the sword. It's glowing slightly, which means there's a monster nearby."

"Good," Spike answered. "Remember to keep near the door with the sword. The last thing we want is for this thing to run down through Mrs. Peabody's living room."

"Got it," Karim answered. "We're in the attic and we've pulled the stairs up after us. I'm guarding the door and Tommy is opening the window."

Spike could see the window in the attic pop open. Tommy stuck his face out and grinned, then disappeared back inside.

"And now I'm going to catch this dang thing," Tommy said.

Spike waited, poised for action if plan A didn't work out. She heard muttering and footsteps through the phone. Then the footsteps increased in speed.

"C'mere, you!" Tommy said.

"He's found the gremlin!" Karim reported, voice raising in pitch. "He's chasing the gremlin. What do I do if it comes after me? *Spike?!*"

"Stay calm, Karim," she responded, trying to keep her voice as level and neutral as possible. "It's afraid of the sword." Why did Karim always have to freak out? He was the one wielding their magic weapon!

There was a crash on the other end of the line.

"It seems to be staying away from me," he answered, sounding slightly less panicked.

"You're mine, gremlin!" Tommy yelled.

Spike heard the sounds of a scuffle, and then a series of

bangs. She squinted at the open attic window, and a puff of sawdust had come out.

"That thing is fast," Karim said.

"He tried to bite me!" Tommy added. "Good thing I'm wearing three pairs of jeans, you little demon!"

It was a good thing that Big Tom was still larger than his son. The extra two pairs of jeans had fit perfectly and would protect Tommy from any but the most serious bites—even if he looked utterly ridiculous. But Spike kind of enjoyed seeing Tommy look even goofier than usual.

"Behind you, Tommy!" Karim said urgently.

"I had my gloves on him!" Tommy said after another series of crashes. The thick leather work gloves had been Karim's idea, along with the ski mask. Tommy was basically impenetrable. It wasn't quite the enchanted elf-forged armor that Spike had seen Mad Mackenzie wear in her adventure streams, but at least it seemed to be working. And it wasn't her body risking gremlin bite marks, after all.

Another slam. Another crash. Tommy yelled something angry.

And then, in a shower of dust, the gremlin appeared in the window and fell to the ground. The gremlin was a tiny, man-shaped creature covered in saggy blue skin. It ran in a whir of sharp-looking elbows and knees, its beady eyes glaring at Spike in challenge. It stuck out its tongue at her, toying with her. Spike tensed to race after it, but the monster darted away.

"It's under the porch," Spike told the boys. "Get down and let's flush it out."

Spike circled the perimeter, making sure that the gremlin couldn't get out from under the porch without her noticing. A minute later Karim and Tommy charged out the front door.

Karim was holding the sword carefully downward, just like his kindergarten teacher had taught him to walk with scissors, probably. Tommy was carrying a huge stainless-steel pot in one hand and its lid in the other.

Spike grinned. The three pairs of jeans and three shirts puffed out Tommy's already impressive size even farther.

"We have to get it out into the open." Her hands tightened around the control pad in her hands. It was time for plan B. Her plan. Of course.

Karim advanced cautiously, sword held out in front of him as far as his arms would reach.

Tommy shambled around to the other side, swaying back and forth with each step. "Why can't *I* carry the sword?" he complained. "It's as hot as the surface of Mercury in here!"

Karim had only just ducked his head under the porch when the gremlin streaked out from the other side of the porch. Those little buggers did *not* like magic items.

"Got you!" Tommy yelled as he leaped with the pot. But the gremlin slipped right past Tommy with a tricky side step, leaving the large boy stumbling wildly. His arms windmilled for a moment, and he flopped into a pile on the lawn. Spike raised an eyebrow at him and shook her head disapprovingly.

A moment later the gremlin had run up a tree and was perched in the high branches.

"Go! Go!" Spike yelled. "Trap it up there!" The plan was going to work.

Tommy and Karim ran to the base of the tree, brandishing their weapons. Spike grinned as the sword's purple polish sparkled in the streetlight.

"We're going to get you, you little monster!" Tommy yelled. The gremlin looked back at him and stuck its tongue out, as if daring the boy to try to climb up after him. Tommy just stared up and growled.

Spike pressed the controls on her remote. There was a whirring sound, and then her dad's drone lifted into the air and buzzed its way up to the top of the tree. Her breath caught in her chest as she tapped the controls gently to position the quadcopter directly above the gremlin. The creature looked up, eyeing the device suspiciously and tensing for a fight. The copter had a small tin can hanging underneath it.

Spike would get only one shot at this. Gremlins could survive jumps from almost any height, so there was nothing to stop it from leaping out of the tree and running off. But so far, more than scared or nervous, it seemed to enjoy taunting the kids.

"A tiny bit farther!" Karim shouted. He had positioned himself under the gremlin so that he could see the alignment. The quadcopter hung above the gremlin, and Spike tapped the controls to lower the copter closer to the creature. The gremlin kept glaring at the drone, making what Spike could only assume were rude and quite inappropriate gestures.

"Now?" she asked.

"Do it!" Karim yelled.

She bit her lip and pressed a button. The can flipped instantaneously, unleashing a stream of reddish liquid right over the little monster. The gremlin jumped, but it was too late: The paint landed right on its face, and it fell to the ground.

Karim, Tommy, and Spike charged at the beast, but the gremlin moved faster than any of them. It shot like lightning, past the grabbing hands of Tommy and the flat of Karim's sword. It ran faster than the eye could see—straight into Mrs. Peabody's garbage can. With a metallic clang, the gremlin fell to the ground like a rock, temporarily stunned.

Spike laughed as she ran to the knocked-out gremlin. The red liquid—the jalapeño pepper oil—had blinded the creature.

Spike made a grab for the two-foot-tall gremlin, but it lashed out erratically and bit her arm, leaving an angry purple mark. *"Ow!"* she said, rubbing the bruise.

Tommy rushed over and took hold of the gremlin with his gloved hands. It struggled for a moment, flailing blindly, but in a few seconds Tommy had stuffed the creature into the stainless-steel pot, and Karim slapped the lid on, trapping it inside.

"Little brat really ran me around!" Tommy said. "But we got you, you hear!"

They could hear angry squeals and scratching coming from inside the pot.

Karim gritted his teeth and held on. The gremlin in the pot tried to push its way out several times, yowling the whole time. Then, suddenly, it fell silent. The poor thing was probably scared out of its mind, but this was for the best.

"What now?" Tommy asked.

"Let's try Mortimer's Monsterpedia!" Karim suggested. "I've been dying to try the new Monster Tongue Translator feature they added."

"Whoa, really?" Tommy said.

"Worth a shot," Spike said, pulling out her phone.

"We're not going to hurt you," Spike said into her phone. A few seconds later, the phone let out a series of squeaks and clicks. "We're going to send you to a preserve where you won't bother anyone."

The gremlin's only response was to redouble its attack on the inside of the pasta pot.

Karim hoped this would work. They had a chance to find

out what the gremlin was saying. Though it was pretty obvious to him.

"Maybe we should call the Burbank Monster Control Bureau and see if they'll take it off our hands," Karim suggested.

But before Spike could dial the number, a large black van pulled into the driveway. Two figures dressed in black suits and wearing silver sunglasses hopped out of the van. Karim recognized them as the AppVenture agents who had picked up the basilisk, and they were clearly on a mission.

"What are you doing here?" Spike demanded.

"I should ask you the same question," the man said. Even behind his shiny glasses, Spike could tell he was glaring at the three of them. "AppVenture has contracted with the resident of this house, and since our Independent Contractor failed, they sent us in to finish the job."

The woman stepped forward and looked into the slots in the lid. The gremlin within struggled furiously.

"They have the gremlin here already, Trent," she said. "Though it looks . . . oily?"

"That's pepper oil," Tommy said excitedly. "We dropped it down with a quadcopter and—"

"We can't know the details of the catch," Trent interrupted.

"We could be held liable if you screwed it up," said the woman, whose uniform had the name *Sylvia* stitched on it.

"Let's have it, then." Trent held out his hands.

"Why should we give it to *you*?" Spike asked. "It was *our* catch."

Trent sighed. "What are you going to do? Take it to the clowns down at the monster control bureau?"

"Look," Sylvia said. "You've done impressive work here, I'll admit that. And catching that basilisk wasn't half-bad either."

Karim, Tommy, and Spike exchanged satisfied glances. Karim imagined that Trent was rolling his eyes behind those silver spectacles.

"Tell you what. If you sign up as AppVenture Independent Contractors, we'll take this gremlin off your hands and even pay you for capturing it. Then you'll be on the list to get offered new jobs in this area. We're going to fire that Jason kid, anyway, and we need someone to cover Burbank."

Trent seemed a bit miffed by this but didn't object. Karim guessed that maybe Sylvia was the one in charge.

"Give us a minute to talk this over," Spike insisted.

"Sure thing," Sylvia said. She and Trent disappeared back into the van.

The three stood in shocked silence for a moment. Was this really happening?

"So obviously we're doing this, right?" Tommy asked. "If we earn enough, Elissa and I can go to Adventure Camp!"

Spike nodded. "It seems worth a shot. Worst-case scenario, we just get paid for this job. We don't necessarily have to do any more. Karim, what do you think?"

Karim nodded hesitantly. What Spike said made sense, but he knew how this would work. Once they were signed up, would they really say no to the next adventure? And what would his dad say if he found out what they were up to? He thought for a moment, still holding the lid closed on the pot as the gremlin took another shot at prying it open from the inside. "I guess," he relented. "Let's just be careful about which jobs we take. Nothing too high level."

Sylvia and Trent stepped back out of the van.

Trent scowled. "We've got a schedule to keep, kids. Make up your minds."

"We'll do it," Spike said. "But on one condition."

Karim sighed but tried not to show it. He should have known this would happen. If Spike ever wrote a book, it would probably be titled *Negotiate Everything: The Spike Hernandez Story.*

"Oh? What's that?" Sylvia said.

"We also captured the basilisk," Spike said. "We want credit for that too."

Trent scowled at them, but Sylvia just shrugged. "Sure, why not. Just sign the forms so that we can get you set up." Sylvia offered a tablet.

The three friends entered their info to sign up for AppVenture, while Trent stood around looking bored and annoyed.

When they were done, Karim stepped toward Trent. "Watch out," he warned, handing it to the man. "You have to keep—"

Trent suddenly jerked back as the lid spun and the gremlin leaped out. Karim and Trent both snatched at it, but the gremlin dodged, landed on the ground with a catlike grace, and then made a run for it—right into Spike's fist as she gave it a vicious punch in the face. The gremlin howled and collapsed.

"That's for the bite," Spike said, leering at the creature. A welt was already appearing on its face, with an imprint of Spike's ring raised in relief above its left eyebrow.

"You've been Spiked!" Tommy shouted as he flopped onto the ground next to the gremlin. He pulled out his phone, made his sassiest face, and snapped a selfie.

"That is *not* my catchphrase," Spike growled.

Sylvia grabbed the gremlin by the scruff of the neck and disappeared into the back of the van, where the snap of a cage closing rang out.

Trent nodded in appreciation. "Nice punch. You kids really need to upgrade your gear and techniques, though, if you're going to play in the big leagues. Speaking of which," he said, raising an eyebrow at their purple weapon, "nice sword."

Karim bristled at the comment but didn't say anything. They'd made the capture, hadn't they? Who cared whether they used jalapeño pepper oil, a drone, and a Violet Sparkle Eminence sword to make it happen?

"You should take one of these for next time," Sylvia said, handing Karim an empty Magical Creature Containment Box from the back of the van. Karim hefted the box. It felt pretty solid.

"See you again soon," Spike said as Trent and Sylvia got

back into the van. But they didn't say anything as they revved up and drove away.

"We did it! We did it!" Tommy cheered as soon as the van disappeared. "We rock!"

"We did, didn't we?" Spike said with a sly smile.

Karim sniffed. "What's that nasty smell?"

Tommy pointed at the pot on the ground. "I . . . think the gremlin pooped in your mom's pot," he said, peering inside.

"Crap," she said.

Tommy couldn't stop grinning. Two days after signing up, a notification on the app appeared: *Adventure Ready*. Tommy had jumped on the message as quickly as he jumped into a pool just at the moment when he knew a cannonball would soak as many of his friends as possible.

So here they were, standing in front of a local restaurant that needed help with a *real live monster*.

"This is the place," Karim said. "Vespucci's Heirloom Trattoria. I've been to this restaurant before. Why would they send us here? Maybe we got it wrong." He turned to walk away, but Tommy put a hand on his friend's shoulder before he could get too far.

"No, this is exactly right. And perfect!" Tommy said. "I bet if we take care of the monster, we'll get free food."

"Okay," Spike said, "let's not get ahead of ourselves."

"Whatever. Let's do it," Tommy answered. There Spike went again, trying to ruin his fun. Well, he'd show her. They'd take out this monster, and then they *would* get free food. With that delicious thought, Tommy led them into the restaurant.

A few minutes later, the trio was in the kitchen ready to meet Mr. Vespucci, the owner—an older man with thick gray hair who was yelling at every single staff member who ran by.

"Huh? What are you kids doing back here? You can't see how we make the Vespucci family heirloom tomato sauce, it's an ancient family secret!" he said as soon as he'd finished yelling at one of the cooks about not chopping onions fast enough.

"Isn't it just garlic and cayenne peppers?" Karim asked. Tommy was impressed. Karim always knew random things like that.

"Yeah, okay, whatever," Mr. Vespucci said, glaring at them. "I grew up in New Jersey, I don't know any ancient Italian cooking secrets, so sue me. HEY, YOU! GET OFF YOUR BUTT AND GET THAT ORDER UP NOW!" he yelled at one of the line cooks.

"We're from AppVenture," Spike cut in. "We were sent to take care of your snipe problem."

"Oh, AppVenture, right. You don't look all that impressive," he said, brushing her off. "But whatever. The dinner rush is getting started, and I need that dang thing out of there."

Tommy grinned. The danger was what made it fun. Karim had that *What have you gotten me into?* look on his face, but that was no surprise.

"We can handle it," Spike assured.

"This way," Mr. Vespucci said, leading them to the back of the kitchen. He opened a huge metal door that kind of looked like a vault. Inside was a room with shelves full of food.

"There's a snipe in your walk-in fridge?" Spike asked.

Mr. Vespucci shrugged. "Every night this week the snipe has gotten in and eaten our tomatoes. We need them for our world-famous family recipes, and we sell a *lot* of pasta sauce. Heirloom tomatoes ain't cheap, you know."

"How does it get in?" Karim asked.

"We keep the door closed, but my head chef, Sarah, said she suspected something was in there. One of those snipes. Now, you kids do your thing. I've got a restaurant to run, and those servers start slacking the moment I'm gone."

As soon as the fridge door closed, Tommy perused the shelves. Racks and racks of food. Meats, pastas, vegetables, fruits . . .

"Tommy," Spike called.

"Yeah?"

She glared at him. "We're on a job. You can't eat any of it."

"Ugh. Fine."

CHAPTER 19

SPIKE

Spike's brain immediately went into tactical mode. It was time to win.

"We need to secure the area," she said, checking the door. "The seal seems solid. Let's search to make sure it's not already in here."

Within a few minutes they had checked every box and container, but had not found any signs of the snipe, other than some chewed edges of cardboard in the corner. There was a large box of tomatoes in the middle of the room. It must have been new, because it was still untouched.

"Okay," Spike said. "Next we need intel. What do we know about snipes?"

Karim already had his phone out and was paging through his favorite app. "Let's see," he said as Spike and Tommy gathered around him.

TWO-TOED SNIPE

LEVEL 2 MONSTER

For many years it was believed that a snipe was a made-up monster used to prank gullible newbies at Adventure Camp. New campers would be sent out to hunt a very tricky creature, always coming back empty-handed.

But it turns out that snipes are very real—apparently, they are just invisible. Because of this, many adventurers believe snipes don't exist, and so the "snipe hunt"—a practical joke amounting to a wild-goose chase—was born.

HABITAT: The two-toed snipe eats grapes and lives in the warmer climates of Southern California, Arizona, and the western coast of Mexico.

THREAT ANALYSIS: Snipes are not generally dangerous. The injuries associated with them are mostly the wounded pride of adventurers who fail to capture them. However, they are considered Level 2 monsters due to their very low catch rate.

WEAKNESSES: All snipes have a strong preference for grapes and can't resist using their stealth powers to steal them whenever grapes are available. Outside of grapes, however, snipes will eat just about anything, though this can vary by snipe. In addition, it is unknown if snipes fear magical weapons; however, when the snipe comes into contact with one, it is believed to disappear, for lack of a better word.

84

■ ■ ■

"Here's the odd thing," Karim said. "Its main food source is grapes. Not tomatoes. Why is it eating tomatoes?"

"Huh," Tommy said. "Well, I like grapes and tomatoes, so maybe they can too?"

"True, but it also says their favorite foods vary by snipe," Spike pointed out, already carefully checking the corners of the room for any way that the creature might get in.

"I guess," Karim answered. "Anyway, snipes are supposed to be very tricky. They are expert thieves, and really stealthy. We're going to have to be careful."

They developed a routine as the night went on. When a cook entered and exited the fridge, Spike watched the door, Tommy checked what they were carrying, and Karim kept his eyes on the tomatoes.

Mr. Vespucci was nice enough to give them some jackets that the delivery boys wore in the winter, which was good because it was really cold in the fridge. Spike shivered. What if the snipe never showed up? Would they be stuck here all night, waiting for a monster that didn't arrive, or maybe didn't even exist?

Then she heard a noise.

"What was that?" she asked. There was a scratching sound coming from the very back of the room.

"Maybe it's trying to break in or something?" Karim asked.

"Keep your eyes on those tomatoes," Spike said as she and Tommy went to the back of the fridge.

The scratching was persistent, coming strong for about ten seconds and then stopping for another ten seconds.

Karim said, "Do you think it's—"

"Shhh!" Spike responded. "This must be it. Okay, Tommy, you run around to the back and see if you can catch it. I'll stay here and make sure it doesn't get through."

"Oh, you want to send me into a dangerous situation, requiring bravery and strength?" Tommy was grinning and flexing his bicep "muscles."

"Ugh, stop talking and go! And if you catch it, just grab it, no selfies!"

"Fine!" Tommy said, sulking as he stalked toward the door.

Karim held out the magic sword to Tommy. "Look, I can barely lift this thing. You can use it, I guess. Just . . . don't do anything stupid."

Spike smiled as the sword's purple paint gleamed in the harsh fluorescent light.

"According to Mortimer's, one slap with the side of that and we'll never see it again," Karim said. "Once a snipe gets struck with a magic weapon, it never comes back. You don't need to hurt it."

Spike could hear Tommy's clumsy running as he jogged around outside, trying to find his way to the other side of the fridge.

The scratching continued for a second, and then stopped, just as it had before.

Several seconds later she heard Tommy's feet on the other side. He knocked on the wall.

"I'm here!" His voice came through muffled. "What am I looking for?"

"I don't know," Spike shot back. "A snipe?"

"No snipes here," Tommy said. "Just some scratch marks down at the bottom of the wall. Is that a clue or something?"

"Yeah, probably!" Spike said. "Anything else out there?"

She heard Tommy rooting around in the area.

"Nothing else, really," he said. "It's nice and warm out here. Can I stay on this side?"

"Ugh, no, get back in here!" Spike said.

"Have you caught the snipe yet?" a voice said from behind her.

Spike spun around. It was Mr. Vespucci, standing with his hands on his hips. Behind him, the door was hanging wide open.

And no one had been watching it.

Had she caught motion, just out of the corner of her eye? A flash of claws, or the tufts of a fur coat? What did a snipe look like, anyway?

"Get out!" she snapped. "It's in here. Don't let anyone in or out until we've caught it!"

20 KARIM

Karim had one job: Watch the tomatoes.

He'd chosen the safest task, sure, but he was determined to do a good job of it. Nothing was going to touch the crate of fruit without him noticing. Karim knew the score. Snipes weren't fighters. In fact, it was impossible even to see one. They had the ability to sense where everyone was looking. To a snipe, sight lines were as visible as light and dark. And so they had evolved to avoid being seen.

This made them incredibly hard to catch. But if you were watching the thing they were trying to steal, like tomatoes, they wouldn't steal it. It had been simple enough to come up with a method to protect the goods: Eyes on the tomatoes.

Around him Tommy and Spike were tearing apart the room, looking for the snipe. It was going to be tough, with racks and racks of boxes for it to hide in.

"This is kind of like a reverse basilisk, isn't it?" Karim said.

"Huh?" Tommy said.

"Whatever," Spike said. "Just keep your eyes on those tomatoes!"

He was watching the crate intently, but his mind was still working. Now that the snipe was inside the walk-in fridge, how would they catch it? The wild search that Spike and Tommy had gone on seemed unlikely to work. Snipes were just too wily for that.

After several minutes, Karim could tell that his friends were getting tired. He was starting to get tired too just from watching those tomatoes so closely. He was also starting to get hungry. It was probably good that they hadn't given this job to Tommy. All the tomatoes would be gone by now.

Suddenly, they heard a crash.

"I had it!" Tommy said. "It was hiding behind that jar of alfredo sauce!"

Karim shook his head, but his eyes stayed fixed on the crate.

"Well, it can't hide behind the jar now, can it?" Spike said. "Nice try, though."

Karim couldn't see her very well, but he could imagine the eye roll plenty well.

As his friends searched, Karim tried to imagine what the snipe would be thinking. But with his attention fixed on the tomatoes, he couldn't get into the right headspace. The snipe would be looking at everything, sensing everything, watching their movements as it plotted. To understand the snipe, he needed to *be* the snipe. He couldn't do that with all his attention fixed.

But this job was better. This way he wasn't hunting after the snipe himself. If Tommy or Spike happened to startle it, they could get bitten or clawed in the eye, or worse. Snipes didn't like to fight, but who knew what a cornered one was capable of?

"Look!" Tommy said from behind him. "That box just moved out from behind the rack all on its own!"

Karim heard Spike running back to join him.

"It's not moving now," Spike said. "Are you sure?"

"Yeah, it moved like a foot," Tommy said. "I'm not making this up."

Karim kept his eyes on the crate. Maybe he didn't need to figure it out. He just had to do his job.

"Okay," Spike said. "I'll hold the box. We just need to touch it with the sword. Then it will run away and we'll never have to deal with this nasty thing again. Easy win."

"Shouldn't I just stab it?" Tommy said. "Much easier. I've been practicing with a sword at home. I can stab the box three times before it can move."

"Whatever you want," Spike said. "But you're cleaning up the mess if it bleeds everywhere."

Karim considered this for a moment. Did snipes bleed? And if they did, would they even see it? Suddenly, Karim could imagine the little guy, trapped underneath that box and about to be stabbed, possibly killed. "Hey! Don't hurt it!" Karim grabbed Tommy's arm as it drew back to swing.

"Ugh," Spike grumbled. "You with the conscience again."

"Listen, we don't need to hurt it to finish the adventure," Karim said. "We just have to hit it with the sword. Easy win, right?"

"Karim's right," Tommy said. "I don't really want to hurt it. What if it squeals?"

Spike shook her head. "You're both wimps. Okay, whatever. Tommy, you swing with the flat of the sword and I'll pull the box up at the last moment."

"Okay," Karim said. "Thanks."

Tommy swung, and Spike pulled the box back at the perfect moment.

The sword swished through empty air. There wasn't a flash of teeth, or claws, or a bit of fur. Just emptiness.

Tommy kicked the box over. It was empty.

Karim finally figured it out, but too late. He looked behind the rack that the box had scooted out from and pointed down.

"Look, there are tracks in the alfredo sauce on the floor. They lead up to this point, and then back from away from it too. The snipe pushed this box out to distract us!"

"What?" Tommy said. "Why?"

Spike growled. "That little . . ."

Something bumped the back of Karim's foot. He looked down. It was a tomato.

They all spun around, but far, far too late. The crate of tomatoes was torn open, and every single tomato had been pecked, or clawed, or chewed. The juice that hadn't been sucked out of them was leaking on the floor.

There was a loud knocking on the door.

"What's going on in there?!" Mr. Vespucci yelled from outside. "My cooks can't cook if they can't get into the fridge!"

"Uh-oh," Tommy said.

"This is just too much," Karim said. "I guess we're not ready for real adventures. I never should have taken my eyes off the tomatoes."

Spike shrugged. "Maybe. I don't know. I was sure we had it." She had really thought they were going to succeed. And the little jerk had somehow outsmarted them. Her, outsmarted by a common snipe! It was unacceptable. "The worst is that when Mr. Vespucci gives us a bad review, AppVenture will probably stop sending us notifications for adventures."

"Guy. *Guys*," Tommy said through slurps of his dinnertime Brotein ("Don't judge a book by its cover—judge it by how much it can bench") shake. "Maybe we lost. Maybe we failed. But it was still pretty cool! Don't forget, we got to see an actual snipe! Well, I saw a tiny bit of its tail, I think. A couple weeks ago, what would we have given to see a real monster? And then we captured a basilisk! So maybe we just need more practice before we try again."

"Yeah, that *was* pretty cool," Karim reasoned. "I mean, we'll get there eventually, right? We probably won't get more jobs through AppVenture, but if we keep going to Adventure Camp, we'll keep learning, keep getting better."

"Well, maybe not for this year," Tommy agreed. "But we'll get there, I guess."

Spike shook her head. She wanted to be an amazing adventurer *now*. "How did this happen?" she demanded. "How did we lose?"

"I think it just tricked us," Karim said. "I knew the minute we saw those three-toed tracks in the alfredo sauce that we had—"

"Wait a second. *Three*-toed?" Spike asked. She tried to picture it for a moment. Come to think of it, that seemed right. The tracks had a clear third toe.

"Yeah, three-toed," Tommy said. "I saw them too. What's the big deal?"

"It was supposed to be a *two*-toed snipe," Spike said.

"Yeah, there are a bunch of different varieties." Karim immediately had his phone out and was poking at it. "That's weird. Three-toed snipes are native to the Everglades . . . in Florida. They don't exist anywhere else. What's a three-toed snipe doing in California, thousands of miles away from its usual habitat?"

"Is that why we got beaten? Because it was a three-toed snipe?" Tommy asked, grinning.

Spike also had her phone out and was scrolling through the article.

"Not really. I think we just . . . didn't win that one. It happens." She'd always thought it wasn't supposed to happen to her, but the universe didn't seem to agree.

"I know adventure streamers are seeing monsters outside their regular habitats, but I haven't heard of anything this extreme."

"Um, guys?" Tommy was looking at his phone, slightly confused. "I guess we were wrong."

He turned the phone around to show his friends.

A little notification from AppVenture had popped up: *Adventure Ready.*

Spike grinned. "I guess we get another shot, don't we? Let's not screw this one up."

"Guys," Karim started, "do you think maybe we should—"

"Admit that we're going on this adventure and skip the argument about whether it's too dangerous?" Spike interrupted.

"Yeah, I wanna have another shot," Tommy said. "I want revengeance."

"Revengeance?" Spike asked. "Is that even a word?"

"It's revenge plus vengeance. Twice as vengey," Tommy answered. "And prevengeance is when you strike first, twice as hard."

Spike rolled her eyes.

Karim sighed. "Okay. Fine."

"But this is a new monster," Spike added. "So it is in no way vengeance, revengeance, or anything like that."

"Nürevengeance it is, then," Tommy said. "With that accent thing with two dots above the *u*, to make it cooler."

The table in Spike's dining room was covered in plates, pots, and silverware. At the center was a large stainless-steel pot full of spaghetti.

Tommy shoveled another forkful of pasta into his mouth. Karim was staring at the pot in the middle of the table in horror, while Spike glared at Tommy.

"Tommy!" Karim whispered when Ms. Hernandez had returned to the kitchen. "That's . . . the pot! The one we trapped the gremlin in last week!"

Who cared what pot it had been cooked in? Tommy's body was a powerful adventuring machine, and it needed maximum fuel. He just wished that Brotein ("Giving you the strength to be strong") made a line of protein-rich pasta sauces. Tommy swallowed and spun another bite of pasta onto his fork. "So? This is delicious! Your mom really nailed it this week, Spike."

"*So?*" Spike hissed. "The gremlin pooped in it!"

Tommy shook his head. "We washed it. No big deal." His friends were so ridiculous. The pasta was good. Who cared where the pot had been last week? That was ancient history, as far as his stomach was concerned. "Besides, it's really a cut above this week. You should try it."

Karim shook his head and helped himself to some asparagus. Spike just sat, staring.

"Well, it's a good thing we've been earning some money on AppVenture," she said. "I may need it to get some food I'm not grossed out by."

"Hey!" Tommy complained through a mouthful of pasta. "That money is for Adventure Camp!"

"Yeah, sure. But you have to admit we're killing it," Spike said. "We're catching monsters left and right."

"Well, we didn't actually capture the shadow recluse," Karim said with a grin. The spider in a local library had been a real hassle until Spike ordered a supercharged suntanning lamp. "We just blasted it with so much UV radiation that it ran into the sewers."

Tommy laughed. "It ran so fast!" The spider's shadowy cloaking had been pretty intimidating at first, making it almost impossible to see in the depths of the library basement. But the fifteen thousand lumens of light had stripped its magic away, leaving nothing but spindly little legs and a very scared creature.

"The best part is, I just resold the tanning lamp online

with a funny description and made the cost of it back the next day," Spike added with a grin. She reached into the sauce with her fork and picked out a mushroom.

"Really?" Karim said, rolling his eyes. "Did you say it was new?"

"We only used it once! I said the package was open but it was unused. More or less true!"

"Your favorite sort of true." Karim shrugged and kept eating his vegetables.

Spike's mom bustled back into the room with a plate of brownies. Tommy noticed that several of them were missing from the side of the plate. Ms. Hernandez had another one in her mouth. He'd never seen her eat anything but sweets, but she never seemed to gain any weight. And the sweets seemed to put her in a good mood. She was always kind and gentle and nice to the three of them. *The opposite of Spike*, Tommy thought with a grin. How had that happened?

"Ms. Hernandez, this spaghetti is amazing. Did you put something special in the sauce?"

Spike's mom grinned at him as she grabbed another brownie. "I did! I got some fancy organic meat and spices. And those new heirloom mushrooms my friend was talking about on her food blogs."

Ms. Hernandez looked at Spike, who had one of the mushrooms halfway to her mouth. "Your father finally got a new job and started paying his child support and alimony again."

Spike froze, staring at her mom like she had just sprouted medusa snakes from her head.

Tommy tried to slurp his spaghetti more quietly as the sudden icy look from Spike chilled the room.

Spike dropped her fork, letting it clatter against the plate.

"Mom. Seriously?" Spike stared at her mother, voice tightly controlled. "You know I don't want any of his guilt money, or whatever it buys." She gestured at the food on the table.

Tommy carefully avoided looking at either of them, like they had the gaze of a basilisk.

"It's our money," Ms. Hernandez said calmly. "He owes it to us. It's the law. And anyway, it's just money."

Tommy couldn't understand why Spike was so upset. How could someone be this mad when there was so much good food available? Usually dinner at Spike's house was just plain pasta with a jar of grocery store sauce. Not that Tommy was complaining, of course; food was food.

Karim was sitting perfectly still, but Tommy couldn't help himself. As the mother and daughter stared each other down, he tried to reach for a dinner roll. He would have to be like the shadow recluse, able to move silently without alerting his prey.

"I don't care." Spike pushed her plate away. "Do whatever you want. I just don't want to be involved."

"Honey—" Ms. Hernandez started, but Spike was already standing.

"I'm not hungry anymore," Spike said. "Let's go." She stood and stalked up the stairs, not even bothering to clear her plate.

Ms. Hernandez sighed. They ate in silence for a few minutes.

"Sorry about that, boys," she said when they were done eating. "You go ahead and have some fun with Spike. She needs it. I'll handle the dishes."

"It's okay, Ms. Hernandez," Tommy said. "Thanks for dinner. It was amazing."

"Yeah, thanks," Karim said. He was trying to strategize a way to get out of the house entirely, but it looked like it was too late for that.

Ms. Hernandez just smiled sadly and started clearing the table. Tommy and Karim grabbed their backpacks and headed up the stairs after Spike.

"Is Spike okay?" Tommy whispered.

"I dunno," Karim answered. The last thing he wanted to do was face Spike in this state, but Tommy was behind him, so it was too late to turn around now.

Karim paused and took a deep breath before they went to Spike's room.

"AppVenture," Spike said as they walked in.

"What about it?" Karim asked, walking over to stand next to her. Tommy flopped down on a beanbag chair in the corner.

Spike yanked at her hair in frustration. "It's AppVenture! His fancy new job is working in IT at AppVenture."

"What?" Tommy asked. "Really?"

Spike sighed. "I looked at my dad's Facebook. He got hired by AppVenture."

"Hey, that's cool! Maybe he can get us better quests or . . ." Tommy trailed off as Spike glared at him.

Karim just shook his head. He said stupid stuff sometimes, but even he knew that was exactly the wrong thing to say right now. Spike was breathing hard and Karim could almost see smoke coming out of her nostrils, like she was a baby dragon.

"That's . . . weird," Karim said, at a loss for what else to say.

"Ugh." Spike threw her phone onto the bed in frustration. "As if he hasn't ruined everything else in my life, now he has to mess up the one thing that I'm actually enjoying?"

"It doesn't have to affect anything," Karim said. "He doesn't even know you're using it."

"Yeah, maybe. But *I'll* know."

Tommy seemed to slump in the beanbag chair. "I promised Elissa," he muttered.

"Look, I get it," Karim said. "Your dad sucks—"

"Yeah, Luis is crap," Spike agreed. "Do you know what he got me for Christmas last year? A calculator. For a class that I won't even take until high school!"

"I know," Tommy said. "But can we just do a couple more jobs and take their money?"

"Ugh" was all Spike said. Karim knew that was better than a flat-out refusal.

"We have to make enough so that we can all get to Adventure Camp together," Karim added. "Don't let him ruin that for us too."

Spike glared at him for a long moment.

"And people need us!" Tommy reasoned. "Have you seen what's happening out there this season? It's crazy!"

"Like what?" Spike asked, clearly curious despite her anger.

Karim quickly pulled up the latest Mad Mackenzie video on his phone. "Look what she posted last night."

In the video, Mad Mackenzie was standing on a mountainside, dressed in heavy padded armor—the professional version of what Tommy had worn when they'd gone after the gremlin earlier in the week.

"After catching a Saskatchewan razorback in a video sponsored by AppVenture, I headed to Grand Teton National Park in Wyoming. Today, we're three-quarters of the way up

Grand Teton, the highest mountain in the park, on the trail of an alerion," she said. "In case anyone thinks I'm making this up, here's a video we caught yesterday." The video showed a clip of a fiery-red bird swooping through the sky, and one of Mad Mackenzie's two camera operators diving for cover from its wings.

"Now, here's the thing," Mad Mackenzie continued when the clip was over, "alerions aren't supposed to be in the Tetons. In North America, they are found only in the Cascades of the Pacific Northwest. Something strange is happening this season—monsters are showing up in places they have no business being. Something is pushing them out of their natural habitats, and no one seems to know why. But I'll say this—it makes for some unique adventuring challenges!"

Karim paused the clip. "Aren't you a little curious to find out more?"

"And to earn money for Adventure Camp!" Tommy added, a bit too enthusiastically.

Spike sighed. "How many more do we need to do?"

Tommy jumped up, grinning. "Three, I think. Depending on the level of the monsters."

Spike exhaled slowly. "Okay, three more. Just enough to get you guys to Adventure Camp. Then I'm out."

This was going to be a tricky one, but at least they had a plan.

"Good luck down there!" their new client, Adam, said as they opened the door to the basement. "I can't wait to be able to buy cereal again once you get that thing."

"Thanks!" Tommy and Karim both said cheerfully as they headed down.

Spike said nothing; she just ground her teeth and kept her grip on the handle of the machine. They clomped down the steps into the basement, the sound of sneakers on wood stairs echoing against the concrete walls, three with bookshelves and one holding a bookcase full of what looked like old track-and-field trophies.

Adam seemed like an okay client, just an older guy who wanted his basement back. Apparently, the teleporting weevil had taken up residence in the basement of Adam's house and had been breaking in and eating the poor fellow's food. She could see how that would get very annoying, very quickly.

Spike hadn't signed up for this. She'd agreed to go on adventures with her friends. But now whenever she heard the name *AppVenture*, it reminded her that she was basically working for Luis—literally the last thing in the world she wanted to do. Why did he think that just because he was technically her father, that gave him some right to ruin everything she enjoyed?

It was like when he showed up unannounced at her fourth grade talent show. She had been practicing that stand-up routine for a month and delivered it perfectly. And then she saw Luis sitting in the front row and forgot the punch line to her last joke. Everybody laughed, but for the wrong reasons, and Spike had humiliated herself in front of the entire school.

That was the problem with Luis. It wasn't that he never showed up for anything or never cared about anything. It was that he wouldn't be there for the things that mattered the most and then would appear with no warning when she least expected it, throwing her whole life off-kilter.

"Are we sure this will work?" Karim asked. "What if it just teleports away?" He had been nervous the whole walk over. No big surprise there.

"We talked about this. It says in Monsterpedia that they can only teleport short distances, right?" Spike asked. Usually Karim was so reasonable.

Karim pulled up the entry on his phone.

TELEPORTING WEEVIL

LEVEL 3 MONSTER

Teleporting weevils are beetle-like creatures and can grow up to eight inches in length. Unlike some beetles, however, they are not capable of flight, but they do have the ability to teleport short distances—an ability that they traditionally use to get inside grain silos, no matter how tightly locked they are. Be warned: Weevils are not afraid of magical items like most other monsters. In fact, they are attracted to them.

HABITAT: Teleporting weevils are pests known for raiding farms in the Midwest, but in the modern era they can be found wherever wheat-based food is stored.

THREAT ANALYSIS: They can be a bit of a nuisance, but beyond the shock of their sudden appearance, they are harmless to humans.

WEAKNESSES: The teleporting weevil is very sensitive to electricity—even a small shock will knock it unconscious. Their teleportation is very limited: Weevils can only teleport around eight to ten feet and need five to ten seconds to recharge before they can teleport again. They are able to teleport through most materials but can't pass through barriers of lead, gold, or mercury. Also, their eyesight is based entirely on motion, so they can only see objects that are moving.

MORTIMER'S NOTES: I ran into one of these guys one summer while I was chasing a flame-snorting stallion in Nebraska. I was just in the bathroom sitting on the toilet, pants around my ankles, when a teleporting weevil appeared right in front of me. We just stared at each other for five seconds, and then the little bugger popped out of existence, never to be seen again.

■ ■ ■

Karim took a deep breath as they reached the bottom of the stairs. Tommy went first, stomping loudly.

"Hey, weevil, weevil!" he said loudly. "We're here! Go hide." The plan was to get it to hide first so they didn't accidentally touch it without knowing. It wasn't supposed to be dangerous, but Spike sure didn't want it teleporting out in front of them. It was bad enough when they went after the invisible snipe. A monster that could literally teleport was a whole new level of creepy.

Karim stepped forward and laid the magic sword on the concrete slab in the middle of the basement.

Spike stepped carefully to the wall, expecting at any moment to feel the touch of a creepy beetle thing appearing behind her. But the teleporting weevil seemed to be in hiding.

Upstairs, they'd seen the evidence that the weevil was around. Adam's whole pantry had been raided. Boxes of pasta ripped apart, cereal spilled all across the floor. He claimed that he'd seen it eating a hole in a bag of flour the night before, but it must have teleported before he got a good look. Spike plugged in the device.

"So it's supposed to be attracted to the sword," Karim was explaining to Tommy. "Unlike most monsters, teleporting weevils actually are attracted to magical items. Probably because they can teleport out of danger, so they're not threatened by weapons and so they don't need to avoid—"

Spike stopped paying attention as Karim went into his theories about monster adaptations. They'd come up with this plan yesterday while Tommy was complaining to the cafeteria ladies that there were no meal options for what he called "protein-etarians." She wasn't sure if he was claiming it was a religion or a health need, but either way, the cafeteria ladies weren't having it.

Spike had to admit that Karim's idea was pretty solid. She pressed the button and the fog machine started up. Tommy's sister had used it for her last birthday party, and when she heard why they needed it, she was only too glad to help. The price, of course, was that now Tommy's little sister knew their plan to earn enough money for Adventure Camp. Spike hated letting someone know about a goal before it was completed, but there had been no way around it.

Spike stepped to the sword as the fog machine started working, at first pouring fog out onto the floor and then slowly blanketing it.

The three friends crouched in a triangle around the magical sword. Spike grinned, looking down at its purple sparkles.

put her through, and how he kept butting into her life no matter what she did.

Suddenly, her attention was drawn away from stewing in her rage. There was movement by the bookshelves. Trailing through the smoke, something had emerged from behind a trophy at the bottom of the case.

It was incredibly odd, seeing the ripples made in the smoke as the creature cautiously advanced. As the weevil moved forward, Spike noticed that all three of them were holding their breath.

The creature reached them and paused only inches from Karim. His zapper was perfectly positioned to strike, but he stayed as still as a gargoyle in the daylight.

"Do it," Spike whispered, trying to move her lips as little as possible.

"But what if it . . . but what if . . ." Karim muttered, his wide eyes staring at the thing creeping along right next to his leg.

This was ridiculous. Karim's timid nature was going to cost them this adventure. Didn't he realize the sacrifice she was making?

Spike raised an eyebrow and glared at him. Karim stared back blankly, eyes wide. Finally, she had had enough.

She jumped forward in a burst, swinging her zapper at the creature. She thought she had been quick, but the weevil was quicker. The zapper swung down, struck the bare concrete floor, and broke in half. The smoke contracted in the

The purple perfectly matched her nails, but i
lous on the sword—and it annoyed Karim and 'i
was what really mattered.

"The weevil only sees through motion. If we
move at all, it won't see us and will come out." Karim
them each a bug zapper that looked kind of like a i
racket. "Wait until it gets close, then try to zap
Monsterpedia says it can't fly, so we should be able to tr.
it by working together."

"It will probably teleport away," Spike explained, even
though they'd already gone over this once before. Tommy
could be a bit forgetful. "But once it teleports, we'll see from
the movement of the fog where it teleports. Then we have five
to ten seconds to catch it."

"Are we going to kill it?" Tommy asked, looking at the
tennis-racket zappers with his brows knit together. "That
seems mean. It's not actually a danger to anyone!"

"No, the shock will just stun it." Karim gestured to the
Magical Creature Containment Box that they'd gotten after
the pasta-pot incident. "That's why I had you bring that. It's
lined with gold so the weevil can't teleport out."

"Okay." Spike glanced at the walls. "Let's just get this
over with."

They waited in silence for several long minutes. In the
corner, the smoke machine whirred away, and the fog on
the ground thickened. As the wait stretched on, Spike tried
not to grind her teeth too badly. She had to focus on doing
this for her friends, not on Luis and the annoying stuff he

spot where the weevil had been, like an explosion in reverse. It had teleported away.

They all glanced around the room. On the other side of the room, she could see what looked like a rippling shock wave in the smoke. It was near the trophy shelf, just about eight to ten feet from where it had been a moment before.

From her knees, Spike looked up and saw Tommy charging toward the weevil.

"Five seconds!" Spike yelled.

It was Tommy Time. Time for fast action. Time to zap this weevil's butt with . . . however much power four AA batteries gave him.

The weevil's outline in the smoke faded away, leaving a trail through the gray fog on the floor. Tommy jumped after it, but the weevil was just too fast.

"Four!" Spike yelled. She and Karim were up now, each coming at the creature from a different direction.

The weevil skittered away from Tommy, and for a second it looked like Karim actually had a shot at it. But he slid a bit too far on the smooth basement floor and missed by inches.

"Three!" Spike shouted. The weevil darted toward the trophy case, but Tommy had circled around and was in its way. He started his zapper in a long sweep along the ground.

And then, suddenly, the creature lifted off and was sailing through the air. It kept going up and up, sailing clear over

Tommy's head. He lifted his zapper to take a swipe, but the weevil was already too far out of reach.

"Two!"

Now this truly *was* Tommy Time. One last chance. He jumped forward, extending his zapper for the final blow. He could feel the zapper whiffing as the weevil reached the trophy case and hid behind one of the large cup-shaped trophies on the second shelf. All Tommy needed to do was grab the trophy and swing his zapper in one smooth movement . . .

"One!" Spike's voice came from behind him.

It was then that Tommy realized he was going too fast. He tried to pull up, but it was too late. He twisted as he smashed into the bookshelf and landed with a thud on the floor.

The golden cup fell to the side just as the weevil disappeared with a pop. Their five seconds were up.

Time seemed to stand still. The shelf teetered back, then forward, and a shower of track-and-field trophies and medals rained down on him. He covered his head with his hands and pushed himself backward, only pausing to look at the case when he was on the other side of the basement.

The bookshelf started leaning to the left and then collapsed, a cloud of sawdust mixing with the fog that was roiling on the ground.

They sat for a long moment in the wreck of the basement. There was the squeal of a hinge, and a figure stood outlined by bright light at the top of the stairs.

"What did you do?" Adam demanded. "What—*my trophies!*"

In an instant, he was charging down the stairs and grabbing trophies, examining the damage. Most were unharmed, but Tommy could see at least one where the man with the javelin had snapped right off the top.

"These took me a lifetime to earn!" the man exclaimed. "Did you know that I was an Olympic athlete? I got a silver medal in the javelin! That medal had better not be scratched—"

"We're sorry!" Karim squealed.

"We can fix it!" Tommy protested.

"Maybe the falling bookcase killed the weevil?" Spike suggested.

"Just GET OUT!" Adam roared. *"OUT!"*

Tommy stayed silent as Spike tried to sweet-talk the guy, but it was no use. He practically pushed them up the stairs, barely giving Karim time to grab the fog machine.

"I'm going to call Sword Squad, even if it costs a lot more," the old man grumbled as they trampled up the stairs. "I don't know why I trusted that slick-talking boy on the internet. I never should have let my niece set this up."

Spike said, "Do you want us to—"

"No, I think you brats have helped enough!" Adam said. *"Out!"*

They slunk out the front door together. Behind them, Tommy could hear the old man grumbling and yelling all the way from the street.

"It flew!" Karim whined as they made the slow walk to the bus stop. "Monsterpedia said it couldn't fly!"

"It didn't fly, it just jumped really high!" Spike shot back. "And if you had zapped it when you got the chance, none of this would have happened."

"Maybe if you hadn't jumped at it from across the room, I would have!" Karim answered, hunching his shoulders and gripping the straps of his backpack tightly.

Tommy cringed. This was not good. "Look, guys, I'm the one who knocked down the bookshelves. It's my fault, if it's anyone's."

Spike and Karim kept squabbling for several minutes. Tommy tried to step in and defuse things, but it seemed like they just wanted to be mad at each other.

Finally, they lapsed into silence until they reached the corner where Karim would head in the other direction.

"Look," Spike said. "This was a hot mess. Let's just take a day off. I don't think I can do this AppVenture stuff anymore. I need to be alone for a while. I'll see you guys on Monday."

"Whatever," Karim said, stalking off toward his house.

Tommy walked with Spike for another few minutes in icy silence.

"Okay, uh, see you Monday," he said when they reached the turn onto his street.

"Yep," Spike said, and walked away.

Karim leaned forward, grinning. "Oh, cool! Mad Mackenzie is streaming again!" If anything would distract Spike from the waves of rage that he was sensing from her, this was it.

Over the weekend, Karim's anger had cooled, but Spike's seemed just the same. She had insisted that she was done with AppVenture, but Karim and Tommy had come up with one last plan to try to get her back in—watch some adventure streaming together. Maybe seeing someone else at it would spark her interest again.

He pulled up the live stream, and they all gathered around the tablet to watch.

"Crikey! And *that*, mates," Mad Mackenzie was saying, "is why you never yank a griffin's tail. Nasty beast, that. Also, don't forget to follow and subscribe!"

On-screen, Mad Mackenzie was driving her Jeep along a coastal highway. Probably somewhere near Seattle, where she lived. Karim wasn't entirely sure why she had an Australian accent, but it seemed to work.

"I was scared going after that griffin, sure," she continued as the trees whizzed by. "There's always that voice in your head saying to run away, to let somebody else take care of this one. But that's the fear talking. You can choose to listen to the fear or ignore it."

Karim nodded. Mad Mackenzie always seemed so fearless. It was cool to see that she got scared, the same as he did.

"Anyway, enough story time," she finished. "We're here. I've got reports on a fresh monster sighting, right here in Chambers Bay golf course in Washington. Apparently, a gremlin has been sabotaging golf cart parts for the past two days, and this morning it somehow drove off with an entire cart."

"Yikes," Karim said with a cringe.

"Let's hope it doesn't mess with our Jeep!" Mad Mackenzie added. "This is why I had it reinforced after the incident with the acid chameleon last fall. It should be basically grem-lin proof at this point."

"Psh," Spike said. "We captured a gremlin just last week. No big deal."

"Yeah, and on our first official adventure!" Tommy added.

"Quiet!" Karim said. "Just watch. I bet we can still learn something."

"Whatever," Spike said. "I'm going to start my homework."

While Spike sat back and muttered about her geometry, the boys watched Mad Mackenzie put her camera drone into the air and head out onto the dark golf course to hunt down the gremlin. Karim wished he'd thought of Mad Mackenzie's drone trick. The drone had a camera and would automatically follow her wherever she went, live streaming the whole way. She had been the first live casting adventurer to do it, but now all of them had gadgets following their exploits. They watched as Mad Mackenzie used an encyclopedic knowledge of gremlin lore to track it through the course.

"She is so good. How does she know how to track it so well?" Karim asked. "I would never have thought to look for engine grease markings to track it, but it makes so much sense."

"No worries, bro," Tommy answered. "We'll get there. Though I do wish we had a sweet ride like hers."

"Yeah, only four more years until we can drive, right?"

"We'll have to do a heck of a lot of AppVenture quests to afford anything better than the twelve-year-old Subaru my dad promised me," Tommy said.

Spike just shook her head and returned to her homework while he and Karim watched the stream.

"Wait a second!" Tommy said excitedly, pausing the video. He rewound it and played the last few seconds. He paused it again and, finger shaking, pointed at the gremlin on the screen.

Karim leaned in, squinting. "Wow," he breathed. "Spike, you're going to want to see this."

"So what?" Spike demanded. "She's caught the gremlin. Good for her." Couldn't they see she was trying to work? And was also super mad? They should know by now to just leave her alone.

Karim shook his head and pointed. "No, look closer. Tommy, I can't believe you caught that!"

Spike leaned closer. What were these idiot boys talking about?

Then she saw it.

"Wow. I'd know that nicely shaped dent anywhere," she said. "I left the same one on that eighth grader who tried to steal my ice cream sandwich." It was the impression of her grandmother's ring. At this point, it was the one thing her father had given her that she hadn't thrown away.

"It's the gremlin we caught from Mrs. Peabody's place," Karim said. "It has to be!"

"That's a pretty crafty gremlin!" Tommy exclaimed. "How do you think it escaped?"

How could Tommy be so smart to catch this, and yet not understand what he was seeing? He was pretty observant half the time, and ignored the obvious the other half.

"I don't think it escaped," Spike said. "I think those jerks who work at AppVenture released it. That must be why they insisted on taking it off our hands."

"Why would they do that?" Tommy asked. "Capturing monsters is, like, their whole thing!"

Spike sighed and grabbed her laptop. "Exactly," she said as she started typing. "Profit motive. The more monsters in the wild, the more people call adventurers with their app, the more money they make."

"Oh," Tommy said. "That's not cool. Not cool at all."

"That's insane!" Karim looked perplexed. "But . . . it *would* explain why there have been so many more monster incidents this spring. If someone was catching them and then releasing them again . . ."

"Like how when I was in my lemonade business," Spike said, "I wanted to go around breaking air conditioners so people would really want a refreshing lemonade."

"Um, that sounds super illegal," Karim said.

"Well, I didn't do it! Mom talked me out of it." Spike was already on her computer, checking facts and figures with other people on chat. "I decided I wanted to win by being better than everyone else, not by cheating."

"But is that really what they're doing?" Karim scratched his ear, thinking it over. "Gremlins are good at sabotaging technology. That's kind of their whole thing. It could have escaped, right?" he asked.

"Karim, you have *got* to stop believing in the basic goodness of people," Spike said. "Tommy, can you send me that selfie?"

Tommy jumped up. "I thought you'd never ask! Um. Which one do you want?"

"The one of you and the gremlin, dummy." Spike sighed as she kept tapping at her laptop.

At least I'm doing something, Spike thought as she went to work. And, of course, her dad would finally get a job and it would be working for a crook like Mike Tuckerville. She should have known not to trust Tuckerville and his smarmy hoodie and tie from the start.

Karim continued watching Mad Mackenzie's live stream. On-screen, Mad Mackenzie was back in her Jeep, holding the captured gremlin in a crazy contraption. "That's a little more sophisticated monster trap than our pot," Karim said.

"Lads, this is a triple-reinforced titanium cage," Mad Mackenzie said. "It only unlocks with my retinal scan. This little bugger is not going anywhere, even if what you folks are saying in the chat is true."

Spike felt the snoring sound behind her, the one that Tommy made whenever he was annoyed.

"You took me out of the pic!" he said. "I sent you my selfie and *you took me out of it!*"

Spike shrugged. "I didn't want your picture spread all

over the internet because of this. Believe me, you don't want that noise."

She smiled, admiring her work. She'd posted it to Mad Mackenzie's Twitch stream chat, along with a screenshot from Mad Mackenzie's gremlin capture, showing the perfect match. The chat was full of other adventure fans calling her a liar and a fraud. But there were a few who believed her.

"Karim. That thing Mad Mackenzie just said. She was mentioning *us!*" Tommy started to jump up and down, shaking the floor. Ms. Hernandez yelled something from below about not breaking her house, and he stopped. "We're flippin' famous!"

"I can see that." Karim turned to Spike. "What are you doing?"

"Spreading the hard truth," Spike shot back. "The thing no one wants to hear. Life's not all fun monster hunts and easy money. The system is busted." They'd see. They'd all see.

"We should have talked this through before we jumped in." Karim shook his head. "Who knows what could happen?"

"And then what?" Spike demanded. "You would have said you didn't really want to do it? And then no one would know about this!"

"Or we'd have planned it out. Figured out how to do it smarter!" Karim shot back.

"No, I had to do it immediately, or you would have chickened out," Spike said. "Like you always do." She knew it wasn't a very nice thing to say. But it was true, wasn't it?

Why shouldn't she be able to say something that was true just because it wasn't nice?

Tommy stood up. "Maybe we should leave her alone for a bit."

Spike looked at him and nodded thoughtfully. Since right now she was furious at pretty much everyone and everything, that was probably the smartest thing he'd said in a while.

"Okay, sure," Karim said, grabbing his backpack from the bed. "Are we going to try that monster hunt from AppVenture tomorrow?"

Tommy pulled out his phone and pulled up the app. "There's still an adventure available."

Spike glared at them both. "That company is corrupt. How can we keep adventuring if we know they'll just release the monsters back into the wild?"

"We *don't* know they do that for sure!" Karim responded. "Anything could have happened with that gremlin."

Spike looked at them sadly and sighed. Were they really that naïve? "Maybe it's true, maybe it's not. I'm not adventuring until we know for sure. And even then—"

"Come on, Karim," Tommy said with a shrug, and led the way down the stairs with Karim trailing behind him.

Spike sat for a long moment after they'd gone. AppVenture had made life so much fun for a week. And now her dad and that imbecile Mike Tuckerville had taken that away from her. Well, if they could take away something she loved, was she just going to sit there and accept it?

No. No, she was going to take something from them.

A few minutes later she was curled up in bed with her laptop, shoulders set in concentration. Her fingers flew over the keyboard as she spread the word across forums and chat rooms, and recruited others to her cause. She was going to blow this thing wide open.

Even if she could never seem to tell her dad how she really felt.

Well, this would show him, at least.

"She'll be fine," Tommy said. In response, Karim put a fork holding a single pea into his mouth.

The two were at their usual table in the cafeteria. Karim was just pushing his food around on the tray, though Tommy had destroyed his own meal with a vengeance and was slurping on one of his ridiculous Brotein ("It may cost an arm and a leg, but your remaining arm and leg will be totally ripped") concoctions. It was supposedly chocolate but looked like goo left behind in the tracks of the notorious bog lurkers of the Louisiana bayou.

"You think so? She seemed pretty mad." The only thing Karim had heard from her was a request to run an analysis of the Federal Monster Administration's monster sighting data for the last year. He'd wanted to talk to her about why she was asking—but once he got started on the analysis he got a bit distracted. It was a good puzzle, and he'd been able to get all the data to make sense.

It turned out that there were monsters showing up all out of place, and usually a week or two after one had been confirmed caught somewhere else. But after he sent it over to her he didn't hear anything back. She hadn't even been in Karim's math class that morning.

"Yeah, this is really not good," Tommy said. "I was hanging out at Spike's house when her dad came to visit last year. She was . . . let's just say she was really not fun to be around. Like, the most not fun you can imagine. Really lashing out at everyone. Some of the things she said . . . I got out of there as fast as I could." Tommy took a deep slurp of his shake.

Spike still laughed at Tommy and his protein and workout obsession. But if Karim was honest with himself, over the past month something about Tommy was starting to look a little more . . . muscley. Maybe this whole exercise thing had something to it after all. Karim was still not quite convinced.

They sat quietly for a moment, with only the sounds of kids at other tables and the occasional slurp from Tommy. And then, seemingly out of nowhere, two hands slapped down on the table, and Spike slid into a chair a moment after.

"Where were you this morning?" Karim asked.

"Doesn't matter," Spike said. "They think I was sick, or whatever. Anyway, we need to go on more adventures."

"What, just like that?" Karim demanded. "You just roll back in and we're supposed to play along and do what you say?"

Spike brushed him off. "We need more evidence. A few people believe me, and they're gathering data. But most of them are saying we're wrong, just making things up. I have to catch and ID some monsters. I've been posting about it, but on the official AppVenture forums they just delete all the posts about it."

"I totally want to catch more monsters," Tommy said. "I haven't earned enough money for camp yet. But what about all that stuff you said last week?"

Spike shrugged. "Sorry, I guess. Can we just forget it?"

Karim sighed. "You bailed on us! We had an adventure reserved. Tommy had to cancel it."

"Yeah, well, it's a good thing you didn't go on it. You probably would have gotten yourselves killed. That would suck." Spike paused for a moment. "Seriously, though. Don't do that. I would be super bummed."

Karim looked down at his plate and thought it over. Was that all the apology they were going to get?

"How do we know you're not just going to bail on us again?" Tommy asked.

"He has a point," Karim said. It wasn't fair, Spike freaking out on them and then expecting to come right back like nothing had changed.

They sat staring at one another in angry silence for a minute as lunch ended and the cafeteria began to empty out. The table suddenly buzzed, and everyone looked down at Tommy's phone.

"It's . . . a video call . . . from AppVenture," Tommy said. He just sat there, dumbly staring at it.

"Well, pick it up!" Spike said, and Tommy hesitantly hit the button.

Spike and Karim crowded around. The screen flickered for a moment. And then there he was, resplendent in his hoodie over a business suit. Mike Tuckerville.

Tuckerville raised an eyebrow. "Are you Thomas Wainwright? You look . . . young."

Tommy glared back at the face on the phone. "I just *look* young! This camera doesn't have enough megapixels to capture my beard. And look at these muscles!" He flexed.

"Look, punk," Tuckerville began, "I pulled your file. I know that it was you who captured that gremlin and then posted it online." The man leered at Tommy, the look of a killer if Karim had ever seen one.

"I, uh, I don't know what you're talking about," Tommy said, stumbling over the words.

Tuckerville shrugged, then adjusted his tie with a sneer. "Sure, sure you don't. Just leave off, and we won't have a problem. Or keep going, and we will have a big, big problem."

"Um, what sort of—" Tommy started, but Tuckerville plowed ahead.

"Just shut it down. Tuckerville out, losers," the CEO said, and his picture disappeared.

Karim was frozen in place. Had that really happened? This was it. They never should have tried to go on adventures. They were screwed, screwed, screwed.

"We've got to bail," Karim said. "Delete the app, hide the money. Never talk about it again. AppVenture? What's that? Never heard of it." He knew he was babbling, but he couldn't stop. This could go so, so badly. "What were we even thinking starting with this? Are we really that big of idiots?"

"Karim," Spike said calmly. "Chill."

He stared at her blankly. "Um, okay." He took a deep breath, trying to gain some measure of focus. "I am now chill. I am relaxed. And I quite calmly think that we have *really* screwed up. Okay, I'm actually not very chill. I don't really do chill at times like this. Sorry."

Tommy was staring at the phone, even though it just showed the home screen, which was technically a selfie of the three of them. But most of the frame was Tommy's face; Spike was frowning at him, and Karim looked like he was thinking about something else and had no idea what was going on.

The cafeteria was empty now except for the custodian, newly thawed from being turned to stone, starting the slow work of cleaning up after the disaster zone that middle school lunch left behind. Normally, right now Karim would be freaking out about how they were going to be late for class. But this seemed a lot worse than just a tardy mark.

"Tommy?" Spike asked, tapping him on the temple. "Is anyone left in there, or did Mike Tuckerville blast it all out?"

Tommy turned slowly. "I hate him. I hate him so much. Maybe we should use the money we've earned so far to buy a ticket to San Francisco so that I can punch him in the face."

"Would that solve the problem?" Spike asked.

"It would solve the problem of Mike Tuckerville not having been punched in the face," Tommy shot back.

Spike sighed. "That might be satisfying for a minute. I can't say I would mind seeing that. But it would be even more satisfying to win."

Karim looked at her in shock. "Win? It's game over!"

Was Spike crazy? He supposed he already knew the answer to that one. Was there even a point in asking questions like that?

Spike shrugged. "Maybe. Maybe not. Depends on how good a plan we can come up with. What can you think of? If, just imagine for a minute, we kept on fighting."

Karim shook his head, trying to clear out the cloud of ideas that was starting to form. He couldn't help it; wacky ideas just came to him.

"Don't try your Jedi mind tricks on me," he said, standing up from the lunch table. "I have to go to class."

"Okay, okay," Spike said. "Let's talk tonight. It's our usual video game night at your place, right?"

"Uh, yeah, I guess so," Karim said. He stopped for a moment, a thought hitting him. "Just don't do anything else until then, okay?" Karim asked. He knew it was the best he could hope for right now. He just needed to be sure Spike wouldn't go right on the internet and get them in even deeper.

CHAPTER 29

TOMMY

Video game night! It was the best night of the week. Tommy just hoped there wouldn't be too much time spent talking. Those robots weren't going to plasma blast themselves, after all.

Tommy hopped off his bike and walked it up the driveway, with Spike just behind him.

"I wish we could tell Mr. Khalil about our adventures," he said. Even though he'd seen Mr. Khalil a bunch of times, the guy was still a living legend.

"No flippin' way," Spike answered. "Karim would probably snap and dye his hair blue and start listening to emo music. Which would be kind of a fun experiment to run. On second thought, maybe go ahead and—"

"Okay, okay, I won't do it," Tommy said as he rang the doorbell.

A few minutes later they were in Karim's living room, sitting in front of the Khalils' big living room TV. The video game controllers that they usually would fight over (the new one was *way* better, and it was definitely Tommy's turn) were sitting ignored on the coffee table.

"Sure you don't want to play some *FIFA*?" Karim asked nervously.

"No, we need to talk about this," Spike said. "We have to go on more adventures. We've got to get more evidence." She grabbed the keyboard and pulled up a series of videos. "People are finding more and more monsters that look similar. There's a one-eared harpy that's been caught three different times—in three different time zones!"

Tommy watched, impressed, as Spike scrolled through the videos. This had started as Spike's crazy theory when she was angry, but he had to admit there was something to it.

"It looks like other people are all over it," Karim said. "What's there for us to do? Besides, you're the one who wanted to stop just a few days ago!"

Spike shook her head. "The next step is to start tagging them, like they do in those shark documentaries. We need to tag monsters and turn them in to AppVenture to get re-released, in order to get solid evidence. Once we have real proof, we can blow the whole thing wide open."

"Are we really going to let Mike Tuckerville win?" Tommy asked. "Are we going to let him intimidate us like this?"

He and Spike had talked about going it on their own, but they had barely finished their captures so far with three of them. They needed Karim's clever ideas. And his dad's magical sword. And, of course, his knowledge of monster lore—the kid was like a walking Mortimer's Monsterpedia, only maybe a little more whiny and scared.

Karim sighed. "Look, I hate that guy too."

"And you're going to let him tell you that you can't be an adventurer?" Spike asked.

Tommy nodded, impressed. He knew Karim, and that was just about the best pitch you could make to him.

Though Karim's dad had been telling him his whole life not to adventure, it was still the only thing Karim ever talked about wanting to do. Other kids dreamed of being a basketball star or a musician. Tommy liked adventuring, but Karim lived and breathed it—even if he was less likely to put himself in danger. It was in his blood.

"Aren't you guys worried what might happen? What if this all goes completely wrong?"

"That's the fear talking," Spike said. Tommy smiled. Quoting Mad Mackenzie was another good way to get Karim's spirits up.

Karim took a long look at both of them, then straightened up. "Okay. Let's at least look at the options, maybe. I guess . . . yeah, it's like Mad Mackenzie said. Can't let the fear be in charge."

They started strategizing from there. Spike put a map up on the big screen, and they popped in all the sightings that had been reported by adventurers who had posted their hunts online. Even as they worked, two more data points came in from the East Coast, where a banshee and another gremlin had been hunted down.

It turned out that since Spike's initial comments, Mad Mackenzie had been streaming about it nonstop and was now convinced too. Tommy had to admit, he was impressed. Spike had started something big. Her conspiracy theory had gone viral.

They were elbows deep in the internet and planning, when the floor creaked ominously. A shape came from the front hall. It was Mr. Khalil, moving almost silently in his wheelchair. Tommy's breath caught. Mr. Khalil's slicked-back hair had gone silver since his days on television, but his eyes blazed as dark as ever.

"Dad!" Karim exclaimed. "I thought you were at your club until nine!" Mr. Khalil had started the town's first wheelchair parkour club.

Mr. Khalil glared at him. "So you were hiding this from me on purpose?"

"No, I, uh . . ." Karim sputtered.

Father glared at son.

Karim swallowed. "We're just following along with the online adventurers."

"And how does that explain the gremlin bites your mother found on your jeans?" Mr. Khalil asked, raising an eyebrow. "I knew I should never have let you go to Adventure Camp," Mr. Khalil growled. "Why did I let your mother talk me into that?"

The three kids sat in silence for a long moment as Mr. Khalil's gaze swung across them.

"Okay. So, what sort of adventuring madness have you gotten yourselves involved in?" Mr. Khalil demanded, eyeing the big map on the television screen.

Spike straightened up. "AppVenture. You know who they are?"

"Yeah," Mr. Khalil muttered. "I'm not so completely out of touch."

"We think they're rereleasing the monsters they catch into the wild," Spike said. "Probably to increase their profits."

Mr. Khalil raised an eyebrow. "And you have proof of this? Strong evidence?"

"Well, no, not yet," Spike admitted. "We don't have the smoking gun. But there have been several incidents of similar-looking monsters being sighted around the country."

Mr. Khalil sighed. "So, the usual conspiracy theories, then? People have been accusing adventurers of the catch-and-release scam since the Middle Ages."

Karim stood slowly, muttering something under his breath. Tommy thought he caught the words *fear talking*, but he couldn't be sure.

Karim tapped a button on his tablet. "Look at this, Dad."

They all watched as the screen showed a shaky camera view of what looked like a kid's birthday party, along with a boy's voice.

"There's something coming in the front door," he said. "It's the harpy. Grandma and Grandpa didn't believe me, but I saw it. And now it's here."

An elderly couple was standing next to a table with a pot roast and a birthday cake, as if they'd just been serving dinner. There were scratching sounds, and the boy swung his camera to the door. It suddenly burst open in a shower of wood splinters.

The creature had the face and shoulders of a furious woman, but the body of a bird. She hopped forward, clawed feet scratching on the kitchen tiles. Tommy looked closely and, sure enough, he could see that where one of her ears had been there was only an old, nasty scar.

The elderly man slashed at the harpy with his walking stick and the woman tried to use her walker as a shield. But they both toppled over as the monster burst past them. A child, who Tommy guessed might be their granddaughter, sat strapped in her high chair as the harpy ate the pot roast sitting in the middle of the table. While everyone else freaked out, the baby dug into her cake with a spoon.

They heard the screams of the boy holding the camera. He appeared to lose his nerve and the view changed dramatically as the camera angle swung to the ceiling. They heard the sounds of the harpy messily eating the pot roast as the camera recorded only the whirring ceiling fan above.

The video paused, and Karim turned back to his father. "That harpy has been captured three times by AppVenture.

First in Connecticut, then in Kansas. This video was recorded this morning in Arizona."

"It's still out there," Spike added. "The police chased it off before anyone could be hurt, but it escaped."

Karim looked at the ground. "Should we just sit here and do nothing about it?"

"Someone has to stop them," Tommy added. He certainly wasn't going to let the other two have their hero moments without him getting in on the action.

Mr. Khalil looked at each of them in turn, and then sighed. "Okay, you're right. *Some*thing should be done. But not you kids running in without a plan or gear! Okay?"

"Okay," Karim and Tommy said in unison. Spike didn't say anything, but Mr. Khalil didn't seem to notice.

"I'm going to call some of my friends who are still in the game," Mr. Khalil continued. "They'll figure this out. Handsome Hal and his crew were going to be passing by from a hunt in San Diego, anyway. You can show them all this evidence."

Without waiting for an answer, he left the room, pulled out his phone, and started dialing.

Spike watched until he left. "So . . . he didn't say we couldn't keep adventuring."

"Yes, he did!" Karim answered.

Spike shook her head. "He said we couldn't go in without a plan or gear. We have the gear, and I think coming up with clever plans is one of our strong points."

Tommy grinned, appreciating Spike's usual vague interpretation of the rules.

Karim threw a couch cushion at Spike, but he had a smile traced at the edge of his lips. Tommy knew from experience that it would take a bit more persuasion, but Karim would come around. Their crew had at least one more adventure in them.

Spike eyed Tommy skeptically.

"It was pretty easy," Tommy said, shrugging. "I just made up a name and created a new account, so we can keep going, like we said."

"And they just let you do that?" Spike asked.

"I . . . don't think safety or paperwork are things Mike Tuckerville really cares about," Tommy suggested.

Spike nodded. She could respect that, at least. Paperwork was for chumps.

"That's awesome!" Karim said. "Our best bet to find recycled monsters is going to be AppVenture. We can't take big corporate adventuring contracts and wandering around on our own wouldn't be all that helpful."

"And this way we can tag anything we catch," Spike added.

The three were sitting at the bottom of the flagpole outside school. The day was over and nearly everyone had gone, piling onto school buses or picked up by their parents.

"They did freeze our payouts on the other account, though."
Tommy said, frowning. "That means it's going to be hard to
get the money I need for camp."

"Hm. Maybe we'll be able to make more on this new
account?" Karim offered. "Assuming they don't figure it out
and shut this one down too."

Spike looked around the school. The only kids still around
were the athletes on the fields across the street, running
through their drills for lacrosseball or footbasket. Whatever
they called those ridiculous wastes of time. Her mom was
supposed to have picked them up half an hour ago. She
was, of course, nowhere to be seen. Typical. Her mom had
the memory of a potted fern and a bad habit of not checking
her phone for messages from her daughter.

"Yeah, great. Now all we need is an actual ride home."
Spike hated when it was her mom's turn to drive them home.
Mom was always so sure that she was going to be on time,
and then about a third of the time she just "got caught up in
things" and showed up an hour or more late. Why couldn't
Mom just admit she wasn't going to make it and let them
take the bus?

She looked up and down the street, and then back at the
school, as if that would help. All the windows were empty,
except for the one where she could see Maria Struthers and
Eddie Suarez, who were still frozen in shock. Students had
added hats and drawn mustaches on both of them. They were
due to thaw any day now.

"Should I call my dad?" Tommy asked.

"It's starting to get late," Karim complained.

Before Spike could answer, a shadow fell over them.

"Tommy. Karim. Colleen," Ms. Smithfield, aka the Sheriff, said, glaring down at the three of them.

"It's Spike," Spike corrected her, glaring right back. "I don't know any Colleens around here." Why couldn't the guidance counselor use her proper name? She had never thought she would miss their elementary school guidance counselor with his touchy-feely magical crystal nonsense. At least that man had been willing to use her actual name.

"I've seen you three," the Sheriff said. "On your phones all the time, late for classes, late for school. Thick as thieves, you three. Don't think I don't notice."

Tommy looked up at her dumbly. "Are thieves thick?" he asked. "Like, are you saying I'm a thief because I'm a little overweight?"

"That sounds like profiling to me," Spike added in. "Discrimination. That's pretty serious, Ms. Smithfield. You know Tommy's mom is a lawyer, right? The suing kind. She'll sue anyone for anything."

"Hey!" Tommy said, pretending to be offended. "My mother isn't like that!"

"Yeah," Karim said, emboldened by the other two. "She won't sue anyone. She only sues people if she thinks she can win lots of money."

"What . . . what are you going on about?" the Sheriff sputtered. "You're lucky it's after school hours, or I'd haul you all in to have a good chat about respect."

"I'm, uh, sorry," Karim mumbled, while the other two glared at him. Karim just didn't have it in him to really defy authority, did he?

"Just remember, I'm watching you three," the Sheriff said, and stalked back into the school.

"What is her deal?" Spike asked after the Sheriff was out of earshot. "Why is she always after us?"

Karim shrugged. "It could be because the school has been evacuated three times this year. And we've been involved in every single one of them."

"*Allegedly* involved!" Tommy interjected. "There's no hard evidence we were involved in any of them. Pure hearsay."

Spike chuckled. Maybe Tommy's mom being a lawyer wasn't completely useless.

Her phone buzzed and she glanced down. She growled and shoved the phone back in her pocket.

"My mom will be here in two minutes. Her client kept her late, apparently," Spike said.

"Those crystals giving her a hard time?" Tommy said with a chuckle. "Were they too shiny or something?"

"It's amazing," Karim said, "that in a world with actual magical artifacts, people still fall for that bunk."

"Can it," Spike shot back. Spike's mom sold special "magnetic" crystals that were supposed to enhance people's vital essences. It wasn't real magic, like Sidesplitter. It was just a load of pseudoscience bunk.

Spike stared at the street grimly. Back when her dad lived here, he would always pick her up on time. But it was better this way. Her mom might be late, but at least she showed up. Not like that one day, the one time her dad had been late. So late that he just never showed up and disappeared to San Francisco for the last two years.

"Okay, are we hunting more monsters tonight?" she asked.

"I can't tonight," Tommy said, shuffling his feet and looking at the ground.

Karim shook his head. "Neither can I."

"What?" Spike sounded surprised, but in reality, she wasn't. Not entirely. This was just typical of her friends, her family—everyone letting her down. She would just have to figure out how to win on her own.

Tommy wouldn't meet her eyes. "I have to go see my sister's play," he admitted. "Sorry, Spike."

"And I promised my mom I would help weed the garden," Karim said, speaking so quietly that he was almost inaudible. Did he think that if he said something very softly, she somehow wouldn't be as annoyed?

"Ugh! Fine," Spike spat as her mom's beat-up old station wagon pulled up to the curb. "We'll do it tomorrow."

After the boys were dropped off and Spike was finally home, she practically stomped up the stairs to her room. Why had they abandoned her? She was tempted to grab her gear and go off adventuring on her own. She should leave her useless friends and family behind, and show them that she could do it all on her own.

She grinned. It was a tight grin, an angry grin. But running off on her own . . . that was loser behavior. She knew how that story went. Going off on your own ended with you trapped in some desperate situation, in mortal peril, and your friends had to come save you. And then you had to act all grateful and like you'd learned an important lesson about friendship and cooperation.

That was *not* going to happen to Spike. Lessons about friendship and cooperation were for suckers.

Spike grabbed her laptop. She could wait and keep working on the long game. Mr. Khalil had said they needed a plan, and that guy knew what he was doing.

Karim stared at the door for a long while before he walked toward it. His dad's car was in the driveway. He knew another shoe was about to drop. His dad never liked to chew him out in front of friends or family. No, he waited until they were gone before raising his voice.

Karim tried to close the front door and tiptoe up the steps with the stealth of an Ecuadorian swamp wraith. It didn't work. He had made his way up only two steps when he heard the familiar sound of his father's wheelchair.

"Trying to sneak past me, boy?" Mr. Khalil asked.

"No, no," Karim blustered. "I'm just getting my gloves so that I can go help Mom with the weeds in the garden."

"That can wait. Come into the living room. I need to show you something."

Karim glumly followed his father. He looked up at the TV screen, where a paused picture made his stomach clench.

"Dad, I've seen this a hundred times," Karim protested.

"And it seems like that just wasn't enough to get the message through," Mr. Khalil retorted sternly.

The video was from Mr. Khalil's glory days of adventuring, when every big adventurer had their own TV show and the networks competed to see who would bag the nastiest monster and get the week's highest ratings. Nowadays it was considered too big a risk of lawsuits and insurance, and the adventuring had moved to streaming apps.

On-screen, a young man, handsome and fit, was standing on a rock outcropping. Behind him the mountain air practically shimmered in the dawn, and a light dusting of snow fell around Yousef "the Fang" Khalil.

"I've taken care of the two trolls trying to feed in the den," the younger Mr. Khalil said, flipping his long black hair in the wind. "Now comes the fun part. The rest of the trolls will be coming back from their night's hunting."

He turned and a group of three trolls lumbered up over the ridge.

"And here they are now," the Fang said. He drew Sidesplitter from its scabbard with a satisfying *schwing* that Karim knew must have been added after the fact. Even adventuring, it seemed, wasn't quite exciting enough for TV.

Karim's stomach churned as the trolls advanced on the Fang. They were rocky creatures, a head taller than an average man and with thick stone skin that even bullets couldn't penetrate. Only an enchanted blade would do the job.

Karim had seen this video too many times to count, and

it made him sick every time. As the image of his father danced in and out from the trolls, dropping the first one with a devastating combination of blows, Karim thought of the first time he'd seen this video. At the time, his parents hadn't let him see it. He'd found it on his own, which wasn't hard because it was on every streaming site when you searched for "The Fang" or "Yousef Khalil." Karim had been only six and hoping to find videos of his dad in his hero days. Instead, he'd seen this.

His mom found him hours later, crying in the deep shadows under the porch. The moments that were about to play out had haunted Karim's dreams for years after.

One of the trolls had fallen into a snowbank, and another was retreating down the mountain, howling in pain. The Fang swung around to face the third troll, Sidesplitter swinging through the air. Karim's eye couldn't help going to his dad's foot. He'd watched this moment over and over. The foot caught in a tiny crevice as his dad spun.

Rather than performing a neat pirouette out of the troll's way, the Fang stumbled as he pulled his foot free from the crevice. The troll lunged forward, and Karim found himself rooting for his dad, as he always did. "Come on, come on, come on," the voice said, even though he knew the outcome.

The Fang lurched back and the troll's rocky fists grabbed his torso, and the two plummeted down the cliff. Karim's dad yelled in rage and stabbed at the troll as they fell, blade cleaving straight through the crown of the monster's head and into its neck.

But trolls are as resilient as they are dumb. The monster's mind was dead, but it kept pushing, kept fighting. And when the two crashed to the ground, Karim's eyes were glued to the exact moment it happened: The Fang's lower back landed on a sharp rock outcropping, and crimson blood splashed onto the white snow.

There was screaming and the camera panned wildly as the TV crew ran to help the fallen adventurer. But Karim knew it was too late. His father's spine was snapped in half, rendering him paralyzed from the waist down.

Karim let out his breath in a rush, suddenly realizing that he had been holding it in. His stomach felt like it had been shot through.

Mr. Khalil let out a disgusted sigh, spinning to face his son. "I had a two-year-old kid at home. What was I doing out there trying to act the hero?"

Karim simply stared at him at a loss. Was his father right? Was this adventuring business just a death wish? Why had he let his friends talk him into it?

"Is it worth it, Karim, to live that life? All I cared about were my TV ratings, my fame, the visits from celebrities and the money that came with it. What was the whole point? I was lucky to survive that accident."

Karim looked down at the floor. How could he explain to his dad? How could he make him understand? Did he even want to?

His dad's question tugged at him as the silence stretched on. It wasn't meant to have an answer . . . but maybe Karim had one. Maybe all those other questions were just the fear talking—the fear trying to take control.

Karim looked up, returning his father's determined gaze. He just might have an answer.

"You always start at that part, Dad." Karim took the remote from his father's shaking hands. "But look." He rewound the video to a minute before his dad had hit play.

Two trolls lay dead at the Fang's feet. He stood inside a large cave, lit only by a fire at the back. The camera perfectly caught the flicker of the fire on the Fang's handsome face. Behind him were piles of bones, remnants of the trolls' many victims over the years.

At the back of the cave, a clump of figures huddled together. They had been a troop of Adventure Scouts, whom the Fang had volunteered to accompany on a trip as a publicity stunt for his TV show. After this incident, local parents had demanded that the troop be disbanded.

"Move!" the Fang commanded. "Get out of here! The other three trolls will be coming back soon. You all need to get to safety."

The camera caught each of the captives' faces as they hustled out of the cave, displaying a mixture of terror, relief, and gratitude. The remaining adult leader and several of the boys were crying. Outside, the wilderness rescue workers wrapped them in blankets and pulled them away.

The Fang faced the camera with a self-satisfied grin. "The Adventure Scout troop has been saved," he said. "The rescue teams will airlift them out shortly."

He strolled out of the cave, and pointed down the slope.

"Now comes the fun part. The rest of the trolls have gone hunting. When they come back, I'm going to rock their world."

Karim paused the video before he was forced to watch the accident one more time.

"Dad," he began, turning to face his father, "even though you got hurt, you did come home to your family. And all those people did too."

Long seconds passed. Karim's dad stared into the distance. Was he going to explode? Scream in fury, or whisper in cold rage? The tension in Karim's shoulders built with each moment.

Everything in him screamed to apologize, to take it back—even to run away. But the screen was frozen on the shot of a rescue worker helping one of the Adventure Scouts into the helicopter. He had to stay strong. This mattered. Fear wasn't going to talk him out of this one.

Mr. Khalil drew in a slow breath, then let it out with a sigh. "Do you know how many people I saved in my career?" he asked, voice almost wistful. "Hundreds, at least. Probably thousands. I was good, wasn't I?"

Karim looked his dad in the eye. "You were the best."

Mr. Khalil shook his head. "But, Karim, you're just a kid. How can I let you risk your life out there?"

"What were you doing at my age? You were chasing basilisks, imps, and other low-level monsters," Karim said. "I've seen the biography show they did when you officially retired.

When you were nine you did a solo raid on a slagworm den and came out with an enchanted dagger."

Mr. Khalil chuckled. "I was a crazy little scamp, wasn't I?" He sighed. "Look. If you're going to do this, I won't stop you. But make sure you know what you're getting into, and stick to the low-level stuff, okay?"

Karim nodded. "I know. I'm not a total idiot."

Mr. Khalil started to leave the room, then spun and glared at his son. "Oh, and one more thing," the old adventurer said. "Follow me."

His father led the way into his study, and Karim at first was confused. But as Mr. Khalil rolled to the display case and opened it up, Karim's heart felt ready to explode.

How had he let his two crazy friends talk him into this? Had his dad known all along that they had taken his sword— or worse, was he about to find out?

"I saw you and your friends running around with that sparkly purple sword," Mr. Khalil said. "If you're going to go adventuring, you'll need a real weapon."

Those two idiots had gotten him into this. Now it was all going to fall apart. He just knew it. But despite knowing that, he took a deep breath and stood perfectly still.

His father lifted the replica and hefted it. "Well balanced," Mr. Khalil said, holding it out to Karim.

Karim just stood there for a moment, unable to convince his body to move.

"You look so scared." His father pushed the sword

forward. "Don't worry, you'll get used to carrying such a valuable artifact around."

Karim gulped and took the fake sword, trying his best to look reverent and honored.

"Thanks, Dad" was all he could croak before he turned and fled.

"You were *amazing*!" Tommy said, grabbing his sister in a bear hug. Elissa had not, in fact, been amazing. That wasn't to say that she had been *bad*. She had done a perfectly decent job. It wasn't fair to compare her to his favorite stars in the Broadway musicals that toured through town every year.

The reality was just that Elissa was eight years old and in third grade. And that the gulf between third grade theater and Broadway was large enough to fit Nebraska. Tommy shook his head. The singing had been pitchy, the choreography sloppy and uninspired, and the tiny actors delivered every line in a flat monotone.

"Your solo was fantastic!" he added. To be fair, it had actually been one of the least awful parts of the show. So, relatively speaking, he wasn't lying.

A year ago, he probably would have said something mean, or nothing at all. But since they'd been working together to save money for Adventure Camp, they'd mostly stopped arguing.

"Thanks," she answered, and Tommy stepped back as his parents took their turn making Elissa feel like a big star. The bouquet of flowers that his mom had brought was almost larger than Elissa was. Big Tom was on, his face looking like it couldn't decide between grinning or crying with pride.

Tommy smiled as he stood back and watched the scene. At least Elissa was happy, for the moment. He hadn't told her yet, and he was dreading it.

"You were *sooooo* good up there!" Mom cooed. "Maybe when you grow up, you'll be a famous actress!"

Elissa grinned, glowing under the praise. "Maybe I can be an adventurer in the summer, and an actress in the winter!"

A sigh slipped out of Tommy, and he turned away so that the regret on his face wouldn't spoil his little sister's joy.

On the ride home, Tommy sat in the darkness and brooded. From the minivan seat next to him, Elissa babbled at their parents the whole ride home. She seemed so happy chattering about how one of her friends had almost gotten crushed by a sandbag backstage.

Over the last year or two she had gotten more annoying, and they'd argued more. But he remembered a time when they were little kids and did everything together. Before Spike and Karim were around, she had been his best friend.

As he started to get older and grow out of the kids' games, he'd always tried to make time for her. The only time in her life that he hadn't been there was when Tommy went to

Adventure Camp. Every summer for the past four years, Elissa had cried the entire day that he was leaving. Tommy had consoled her, telling her stories about Adventure Camp and trying to distract her by promising her things he would show her when she was finally able to go.

And this year he had promised her that she would get to go to Adventure Camp.

He reopened AppVenture on his phone, but it showed the same thing: financial account frozen.

Tommy had gone onto AppVenture every day since it was first frozen and tried to cash out the money they'd made so far. But the payouts had been frozen for "account fraud review," and the status hadn't changed for the past several days. Tuckerville hadn't shut down the whole account, but he had locked down the most important part. There was no way to get paid for anything they had done.

At home, Elissa waited until they were alone in the kitchen. Mom had disappeared into her office, and Tommy could hear the TV in the living room. He poured each of them a bowl of cereal, and Elissa was struggling to put a full gallon of milk onto the counter for him.

"What's wrong, Tommy?" Elissa asked. "You've been a sourpuss all night! Didn't you like the show?"

Tommy glanced down at his tiny sister. Could he tell her? That he wouldn't be able to keep his promise, and she would have to wait another year to swing through the ropes course or scream when the counselors sent the new campers through the banshee hut?

"Oh, nothing," Tommy lied. "I was just wishing that we'd had as good plays as this when I was your age."

Later that night, as he poured the milk over some of the most sugar-rich cereal on the continent, Tommy took a deep breath. He was going to get that money, one way or another.

He didn't have any great ideas, but he knew two people who were great at coming up with those. Even if one of them was kind of bossy and the other was scared of his own reflection.

"So the place they're sending us is actually a company, something called MHT Aeronautics," Tommy explained. "For some reason, this is the only adventure that's been available for the past couple of days."

The young adventurers had grabbed the city bus as soon as school was out. Spike was pleasantly surprised that they'd both come along without complaint. She'd half expected them to back out.

"It says there's a fire drake shacked up in an old condemned office building by the airport," Tommy continued. "It's getting in the way of tearing the place down or some junk like that."

"What do we know about fire drakes?" Spike asked. It was best to go in with a plan. Spike didn't like surprises; she liked winning.

Karim was already tapping and swiping at his phone, and soon he had pulled up the entry on fire drakes.

FIRE DRAKE

LEVEL 3 MONSTER

The fire drake is a small crested bird, with an internal body temperature just below boiling.

HABITAT: Warm underground caverns throughout the world are known to harbor fire drakes. They despise colder climates.

THREAT ANALYSIS: The fire drake is powered by a mystical flame inside it that feeds its energy. Their claws are perilously sharp, and given enough time, they can cut their way out of any cage with sheer manic will. Their insides run so hot that their droppings come out scorched, like badly burned sausages.

WEAKNESSES: Purified water will temporarily still the fire drake's energy, making it very lethargic and easy to capture. Unlike true dragons, their larger cousins, fire drakes are not very smart and don't have a real language or true intelligence. But watch out—their deadly talons can be cut only with a magical weapon.

MORTIMER'S NOTES: I kept a fire drake as a pet for a while—after its claws were trimmed, of course. They're great for keeping a small apartment warm when you're behind on rent and the landlord cuts off your heating!

"Mortimer's says that it's a Level Three threat," Karim said.

"Sweet," Spike said. "So how do we capture it?" Her instincts said they should stop doing AppVenture since the company refused to pay them any money, but this was beyond money now. She was just glad it had kept offering them assignments. Well, one, anyway.

"Basically, you just need to douse it in a bucket of purified water," Karim explained. "And then you can hold it while you use an enchanted sword to trim down its talons so that it can't claw you up."

Tommy looked at the picture on Karim's phone and flexed. "I can get it in that hold, no problem." He took out a Brotein ("Winners don't wear sleeves") bar and began eating noisily, almost as if that would somehow make him stronger right now. But if that got him in the right frame of mind, she was fine with it.

Spike leaned over to check it out as well. The fire drake looked like a tiny dragon, about the size of a goose. Sometimes they could breathe a little bit of fire, but she guessed that the water would take care of that.

"And after that?" she asked. "Can we use a Magical Creature Containment Box on it?"

Karim shrugged. "Once you trim its nails, it's just a matter of getting a leash on it. You can pretty much walk it like a dog."

"Okay," Spike said. "So we need a leash and some water." This seemed like it should be fairly straightforward. Maybe one of these adventures would go smoothly, for once. She rather suspected one of the boys would find a way to screw it up, though. They always did.

"The rope in my kit should do the job." Karim patted a gym bag on the floor. "Dad made me put it together after we talked. He said no son of his would go into adventures unprepared."

"I brought a jug of purified water," Tommy said, hefting his backpack. "I read up on fire drakes last night. We're gonna quench that little guy."

Not to be outdone, Spike pulled a small contraption out of her backpack. "Long-range radio frequency identification tag," she said. "We can tag it under one of its scales so we can track it if it's released."

"Great," Tommy said. The bus took a turn, and they all hung on to their seats for a second.

"One more thing," Karim said. "I was thinking about the money problem last night. And now that Spike's alias is getting pretty well known in the adventuring community . . ." He pulled out a phone with a double battery pack on it.

Spike smiled. She already knew where this was going. Karim had nailed it again. "We're going to live stream it," she said. "We can run ads on our adventures and make some money that way."

"Exactly," Karim said.

"Won't that get us in trouble, though?" Tommy asked. "If the teachers or the Sheriff see us doing this . . . heck, or my mom!"

Spike had to admit she was surprised that Karim wasn't the one pointing that out.

"No problem," Karim said. He tapped at his phone for a moment. "We can mostly stay out of the camera and focus on the monster itself. And the live-stream app actually has a face-blurring feature. I'll just turn that on."

The bus finally came to their stop, and as soon as they were off, Spike took the camera and started toward the building. After another minute of walking, Tommy came up alongside her and held out his hand. She looked down at it skeptically and raised an eyebrow.

"Let me handle this," he said. "You have to do it with style and class, or no one will watch."

Was he serious? It did make a typical Tommy sort of sense. Most of the casters kept up a constant stream of words, a sort of verbal nervous tic that she'd always thought was annoying. But that *was* the way things were done. Spike glanced at the camera and saw that the current viewer count was at a very impressive three.

She handed him the camera with a shrug. "Knock yourself out."

Tommy gave her the type of grin usually reserved for Christmas morning and held up the camera.

"This is Tom—um, I mean, T-Bone here," he started. "Man of mystery, adventurer at large, and hero of the hour." As he started to pick up steam, his voice changed into a sort of energetic parody of itself. "My face is blurred to preserve the mystery, but rest assured, gentle stream viewers—I am quite handsome and that dark patch on my chin is the beard I've started growing."

This performance was something that Spike could easily imagine Tommy having practiced before. Probably standing in front of a mirror, or taking videos of himself that he would never show to anyone else. She sighed. It might be stupid, but at least she didn't have to do it.

"So, as I said, I'm T-Bone," Tommy continued. "And today we're going after a fire drake, along with my cheerful and worthy companions, um . . . K-Ram, and—"

"Spike," Spike interjected. "Just Spike." She was *not* going to get stuck with a dumb Tommy nickname.

"And Spike," Tommy finished. They approached their destination, Tommy filling the air with words while Spike and Karim examined the office building. It was about eight stories high, and the lower floors were covered in graffiti. It clearly hadn't been used in quite some time.

"It looks like a mess," Karim said quietly as they let Tommy go ahead. "Half the windows are broken and those walls haven't been washed in years."

"I can see why it needs renovations," Spike agreed. "Though it looks like it would be easier to push it over than to fix it up. But the structure is probably fine."

"Adventure team!" Tommy said from up ahead. "I've found a clue!"

"Um, Tommy," Spike said. "Sorry—*T-Bonehead*—this is an adventure, not a mystery!"

The three grouped around the front door of the decrepit office building, which had a note taped to it. Tommy read it out aloud for the benefit of all three of their current viewers.

Spike leaned in to read it for herself.

AppVenturers! I had to run to find a bathroom where the toilets actually flush. But the door is open and the fire drake is in the basement. Usually Subbasement C, I think. Good luck! Send me snaps on Insta when you're done.

—Salvatore Rodriguez, MHT Aeronautics Maintenance

"Thanks to our new friend, Salvatore, we're inside!" Tommy proclaimed as they entered the building. The air inside was musty and every step kicked up dust. There were a few pairs of footprints in the filth, along with a long, messy furrow leading into the darkness, as if someone had dragged a large piece of equipment through.

"Let's hope he finds the happy toilet he's been searching for," Tommy added.

Spike rolled her eyes. Tommy's broadcast persona was going to get old, fast. But she stepped up behind him and took a glance at the screen. They were up to eight total viewers. She bit back any sarcastic comments. Tommy's shtick seemed to be working, she gave him that.

Spike tried a few light switches, but they had no effect.

"Here you go," Karim said, pulling flashlights from her bag and passing them out. "That'll be a lot more powerful than the one on your phone."

They flicked on the flashlights and advanced into the darkness.

The power being out meant that the elevator wasn't working, which was just as well. Tommy had wanted to try it, but in dangerous situations like fires or monster hunts, it was best not to rely on elevators. The last thing you wanted was to be trapped in a tiny metal box with some magical beast on the loose.

They moved down the stairs to the basement single file, Tommy leading the way with the camera.

Karim turned off his light for a moment, trying to see the place the way that a fire drake would. The office building was the perfect dungeon. Out of sight, and easy to disappear into. He shivered. There was a reason monsters hid in caves and dungeons—it made things that much harder on the adventurers.

"And so we venture into the depths," Tommy was whispering in his new adventure casting voice, "with only our lights, our magical sword, and our wits to protect us from the dangers that lurk beyond."

Karim rolled his eyes but checked the stream on his own phone. Almost a hundred viewers! How were they that popular already? He supposed that active monster hunts were a little less common than the thousands of streams of the popular video games. You needed to have a real-life monster, a magical weapon, and the guts to actually go and do it.

How had Karim convinced himself to get down here? Looking around at the shifting shadows on the wall, he shook his head. This was madness, but he was already well committed now. He just hoped they wouldn't end up in a hospital after it was all over—or worse.

Tommy had the bucket of water held in one hand as he walked with the camera. Karim pulled his father's magical sword out of its wrappings, hefting it. The weight in his hands felt reassuring. It was the same size and weight as the replica that Tommy's dad had gotten him, but somehow holding the real magic one had an extra zing of power. It did still sparkle with purple nail polish—Karim had to admit that it looked kind of cool.

At the bottom of the stairs, they reached the first basement level. The hall diverged in three directions, each as dark as the last.

"Should we split up to cover more ground?" Spike asked.

She looked at the two boys with a raised eyebrow. Karim nodded thoughtfully, while Tommy stroked the few hairs on his chin. Karim, with a chin as smooth as a suit of plate armor, had to admit he was a tiny bit jealous.

"Yeah," Tommy agreed, his face twitching slightly. "Each going our separate ways with no backup sounds like a great idea."

"Yup," Karim added, trying not to grin. "That absolutely will speed things up and not end up with all three of us getting picked off one by one."

Without further discussion, they headed to the left together. Karim smiled. They all knew better than that. Spike's listicle "Ten Ways Not to Be Another Dead Adventurer" last year had been a big hit on social media. This was a clear case of number six.

They went room by room with their flashlights, checking for signs of the drake. Tommy's light pointed in front of them, Spike's shone behind, and Karim's played across the rooms, searching for hints. He'd always been the best at finding clues.

"There are burn marks on those boxes," he said in the third room that they checked. "And claw marks on that wood crate."

They searched the room for anything else, but that was all there was.

After a few steps back in the hallway, Tommy turned with a sour face, and his flashlight fell to the ground.

"Ew!" he said, wiping his feet on the ground. "Um, what kind of poop do fire drakes leave? Are these them?"

"Um. Yep," Karim said. It was good that he had the app

version of Mortimer's Monsterpedia, since there didn't seem to be much service down here. That also meant that their live stream had stopped and they would have to upload the video when they made it back topside. "They look like badly burned sausages." He looked down at the ground, his stomach turning as he compared it to the image on his phone. "That looks about right."

"Yum," said Spike, wrinkling her nose. "But . . . don't they seem a bit big?"

Karim compared the phone with the evidence on the floor again. "Well, they're exactly the right shape and, er, consistency," he answered. "It doesn't say how big they are. They must just be big, I guess."

"I hope we brought enough water." Spike eyed the jug that Tommy was carrying.

"It doesn't take much," Karim answered, recalling the reading that he'd done in Mortimer's. "You just have to put out the source flame at the back of their throat. Toss the water in when it opens its mouth, and you're good."

"There's fire in its mouth?" Spike asked.

"Sounds pretty dangerous until you get it soaked!" Tommy said, looking around a bit apprehensively.

Karim shrugged. "There's a reason they're low-level. They're small, and the flame isn't very hot. They mostly eat grasses and, in cities, wood and cardboard. The flame is really to scare predators away."

They walked the rest of the floor in silence. Karim pointed out several more flame marks and claw marks as they went, but they didn't look fresh. And the droppings that Tommy found were all hard.

Twice Spike halted them. "I thought I saw something back there," she said, frowning. "But with just the flashlight it's so hard to tell."

"Rule number eight," Karim said. "If you think you see or hear something suspicious, stop and make sure it's not going to kill or maim you." It seemed like a pretty solid rule.

They doubled back and searched the area, but couldn't find anything.

Spike ran her flashlight over the floor. "There are footprints in the dust, but they look like ours."

"Yeah, I don't see any clawed feet," Tommy said, looking down. "Looks like it was nothing."

"Or else . . . it was flying?" Karim suggested. "They can fly." It was an odd image, and he wasn't sure fire drakes could fly in such a small space, at least not continuously. He thought they were more like chickens in that regard.

"It would have to be pretty smart to know how to do that," Spike said. "How intelligent are fire drakes?"

Karim knew the answer but still felt the need to double-check. "Monsterpedia says they're a lot dumber than real dragons and don't really have a language," he said.

Spike shrugged. "It's possible that one was flying, but it seems unlikely it would know not to ever land. If it could even do that."

Karim sighed. At least Monsterpedia made it sound like fire drakes weren't all that dangerous. If the biggest prey it hunted were rats and pigeons, he figured that three of them could probably take one down.

"There's nothing here," Tommy said, eyeing the staircase up ahead. "Let's keep moving."

Karim found his pulse beating faster as they tromped down into lower and lower levels of the basement. Each level was more of the same. A few marks here and there, but nothing recent.

Four more times they stopped because one of them saw something in the distance, but each time they found nothing but empty hallways and their own sneaker prints on the dusty floor. How must they look, through the eyes of a predator? If he was the drake, what would he do? Attack them, run from them, or lure them into a trap?

Was the drake toying with them, or was Karim's imagination just running wild in the depths of this building?

Tommy grinned.

Not only was this going to be awesome, it was going to be awesome . . . LIVE ON STREAM.

"The note said it would most likely be here," Spike said as they reached the bottom level of the stairs and a found sign that said SUBBASEMENT C in large block letters.

"Maybe we should have just checked here first, then, huh?" Tommy was starting to get frustrated. They'd been down here for hours now, with no signs of finding the fire drake.

"We do things step by step," Spike shot back, appearing to be a bit snippy herself. "That way we don't die."

Tommy shrugged. He was still annoyed, but it was too late to do anything. They started to work their way down the first hallway of Subbasement C, with the same efficiency they'd been using so far.

He glanced down at his phone. Well, maybe not so much live on stream. This deep underground his phone had lost signal.

They'd been up to two hundred viewers before it cut out. Though he knew from experience that an adventure caster disappearing into a dungeon with no signal was sometimes the best thing that could happen to a caster. Viewers loved to speculate about how dead the adventurers were—as long as they weren't kept waiting for too long.

Tommy had been taking video of occasional moments in the dungeon crawl so that they could post them later, but he'd mostly kept the camera off. This was getting boring, and he didn't want to bore his viewers too much on their first adventure.

"How long do we look before we give up?" Tommy said. He was almost looking forward to admitting that they weren't finding the darn monster tonight. If they left now, he would still have time to do a workout and slam down some Brotein ("Pain is just weakness leaving the body and leaving behind totally jacked biceps") shakes before he went to bed.

"I guess we could come up with a better way to find it and come back," Karim admitted. "Maybe we could use some sort of bait, like a package of ground beef or something?"

"We still have an entire floor to search," Spike said. "No defeatist talk until we're at least done with the whole search, okay? Or are you guys so eager to give up?"

"Hold up!" Karim whispered. "I think I hear something."

Tommy froze, but inside he was fuming. Karim had stopped them several times now, and each time it had been for nothing. Adventuring was supposed to be about charging in!

The guy's imagination was going crazy. Tommy supposed he could understand it. If he were a scrawny little guy like Karim and not a fearless mountain of strength, he would probably be scared all the time too.

They stood perfectly still. Tommy tried to focus over the sound of his friend's breathing. And there was something there. They all turned slowly. Quiet scuffing noises came from the stairwell.

"Maybe the drake circled behind us," Karim whispered.

"Get set," Spike said.

Tommy held the water jug at the ready while Karim drew Sidesplitter and took up a defensive stance. Spike pulled back and held her phone up, preparing to record the action.

They were poised to strike. Tommy was five feet, eight inches of monster-crushing machine. And he supposed that Karim was competent enough.

They waited a few long seconds as more faint scuffing sounds came from the hallway. Suddenly, the door slammed shut and Tommy jumped back, then charged forward. Before he could reach the door, he heard the sound of a magnetic lock clicking. He tested the door anyway, ramming his weight against it. It was solid metal, probably some sort of reinforced fire safety door.

There was a small window, also glass reinforced with wiry lines of metal. A face appeared behind it, framed by a very distinctive outfit—a hoodie sweatshirt over a crisp white collar and tie: Mike Tuckerville.

The tech magnate grinned with a wicked joy, then disappeared as the sound of footsteps running up the staircase rang through the basement.

Tommy pushed at the door, then slammed himself against it several more times. It didn't give, not even a tiny bit. If only Tommy had doubled his Brotein ("When brute strength just isn't enough . . . more Brotein!") intake for the past month, he surely would have had the oomph to bust through it. But it just wasn't giving. Tommy rammed into the door again.

"Tommy—Tommy, stop," Karim said quietly.

"Look," Spike said, pointing the opposite way, down the hall. It was long, probably running the whole length of the basement. At the other end, a massive shape was stalking around the corner, its eyes glowing in the dim light.

Tommy squinted. It looked a lot like the fire drake from Mortimer's Monsterpedia . . . but about five times larger. It was easily eight feet long, a miniature dragon with glistening green scales and a spiked tail.

"Th-that's not a fire drake," Karim stammered. "That's a real dragon! What the heck is it doing in Burbank?"

Tommy couldn't believe it. He looked down at his phone. There had to be an explanation for this. He blinked. There was no service now, but at some point on the way downstairs it must have gotten enough signal to update. Uh-oh.

"Now all of a sudden it says the quest is to catch a dragon!" Tommy said. "A Saskatchewan razorback!"

"That's a Level Seven monster!" Karim's eyes were wide. "Crap, crap, crap," he repeated over and over under his breath. Razorbacks were the smallest breed of dragons, but they were still dragons, and definitely bigger than fire drakes.

"They're covering their tracks," Spike said darkly, glancing around. "It looks like we agreed to this, so it won't be their fault when we don't survive. We agreed to the danger when we signed up."

"Just a few more adventurers who couldn't take the heat," Karim said grimly.

There was a ringing in the air. The kind of ring that Tommy had only heard in his grandma's house. An old-school phone. A landline. It was coming from an open doorway behind them.

"Guys, get that door," Spike said, striding to the phone. "Block it with something."

Behind her, she heard the sound of the door slamming shut, then locking. As she picked up the phone, she glanced back and saw Karim sliding filing cabinets toward the door.

"Hello?" Spike answered.

"Oh my god, Colleen, it's you," the voice on the other side said. "Are you hurt? Are your friends okay?"

The blood that had been pounding in her veins suddenly turned to granite. It was the last voice she expected to hear—the last voice she ever *wanted* to hear.

"The name is Spike," she said quietly. Behind her, the razorback scratched at the door. She spun around and saw that the door was holding, defended by more and more filing cabinets. "But better yet, don't call me anything at all. I need to go get killed in the trap that *your* new employer set for us, Luis."

It was that useless waste of the planet's resources that was supposedly one of her parents. Why was her father calling her down here? How had he even known to? Wanting to know the answer to that question was the only thing that kept her from just hanging up on him immediately.

"Honey," he said, apparently choosing not to call her either Spike or Colleen, "I had no idea they were doing this. I would never put you in danger. They only just told me. I'm so sorry."

"No need for apologies, Luis," she responded. "I don't care what you do."

"Just hear me out," he answered with a sigh. "AppVenture has a rescue team on standby. All you need to do is give them the passwords to your online accounts so that they can post online admitting you made up the stories you've been spreading about us. About them, I mean. You can get out of this without getting hurt."

In the background, Spike vaguely noticed Karim and Tommy yelling something about fire. Spike hit mute on the phone and relayed the offer to her friends.

"They want us to give up our accounts?!" Tommy said. "If they have the password, that's permanent!"

Karim took a deep breath. "This dragon is way out of our league." He closed his eyes, squirreling his face up in that way he always did when he was running scenarios. "I want to get out of here. But if they have our accounts, we have no leverage anymore. They can make it look like this was all our fault. We get eaten by the dragon and they get away unscathed."

Spike nodded. She picked up the phone again.

"Wow, Luis," she said. "Just . . . wow. Now you're helping them threaten and extort me? The people who just released a *Level Seven monster* on three seventh graders!"

"I'm not on their side, honey!" His desperation was coming through the phone. "I just don't want you to get hurt! Please, take the deal. Look, we just flew in from San Francisco. I'll be there soon—I can be there in an hour. After you get out, I'll pick you up and take you all home. Just take the deal, and this can all be over safely."

Spike paused for a moment, looking around the room.

Outside there were scraping sounds as the razorback stalked along the hallway. Then came a loud *whoosh*, and a light flickered under the doorway. Even on this side, she could feel the temperature rising slightly. That thing was a heck of a lot more powerful than a little fire drake. Mike Tuckerville didn't just want to scare them; he wanted to see them roasted alive.

Tommy was hefting his jug of water. Suddenly, it didn't seem like that much.

"The door is starting to char," Karim said, pulling another filing cabinet from a far corner to add to the pile blocking the door. "Another one like that and it will start to burn!"

"Maybe it's like a shark," Tommy said as he dragged the last cabinet into place. "If I just punch it in the nose hard enough, it will back off."

"Or we could just hold its mouth shut, like an alligator," Karim suggested.

Spike took in the whole scene. Her friends were working bravely, but she could see the panic in their eyes.

Mike Tuckerville had them in a tight spot—trapped in a room with only one way in or out, with a deadly magical predator steadily burning its way in to eat them alive. Tuckerville was so sure he could make them do whatever he wanted. He probably thought he had already won.

But Mike Tuckerville was not going to win. Not today. Not if Spike had anything to say about it.

"Luis, you disgust me," Spike finally said. "Oh, and tell your pal Mike Tuckerville that his hoodie looks dumb and his haircut is cheesy. The monsters they're rereleasing are dangerous. If we don't get this story out, more people will probably get hurt—or worse. No deal."

"Colleen—" Luis Hernandez started, but Spike slammed down the phone.

The whooshing sound came again from the other room. The temperature rose a few more degrees, and she could see tiny flames licking around the edges of the door.

Tommy and Karim stared at her, but to their credit neither of them was dumb enough to tell her that she should have taken the deal.

"Okay," Spike said. "Karim, we need one of your crazy ideas. How do we survive this?"

37 KARIM

Karim stood in the center of the room. He tried to take it all in, to consider every resource available to him. Every situation had a set of rules. Every set of rules could be exploited.

This room had one door, one way in or out. It contained nothing other than old filing cabinets, some rolling chairs, and a telephone. Four walls—one gray concrete, three painted a faded white. Outside the door was a giant fire-breathing lizard that was about to blast its way in and eat them within minutes.

Karim looked at the telephone, but Spike picked it up and shook her head. "It's been disconnected," she said. "Tuckerville is not doing this halfway, is he?"

Karim focused. Okay. That was the situation. What else did they know? He pulled out his phone, bringing up Mortimer's Monsterpedia. Luckily it had an offline mode so adventurers could get info on monsters even in the deepest dungeons or wildest woods.

SASKATCHEWAN RAZORBACK

LEVEL 7 MONSTER

The smallest of the true dragons, Saskatchewan razorbacks make up for their relatively small size in ferocity and fiery breath.

HABITAT: The Saskatchewan razorback is found only on the Canadian Shield plateau, in the Saskatchewan province. They have a strong sense of pride and their own honor and importance, and cannot be tamed or ridden by humans.

THREAT ANALYSIS: When they are hungry, these dragons will eat almost anything that moves. When they sense prey, razorbacks ignite the flame sacs in their throats that produce their fire breath. Once the flames are lit, the flame drives them into a hunting frenzy. These dragons will pursue their prey until they are victorious or their flames go out. When this happens, they will usually return to their lairs to rest.

WEAKNESSES: If the flames can be put out, the razorback becomes less aggressive. But it's still a giant armored dragon with claws and wings, capable of ripping a person to pieces if offended.

are extremely dangerous and extremely rude! The last one I met took the
pinky toe on my left foot and really, really hurt my feelings.

■ ■ ■

"I think our best bet is to extinguish its flame," Karim
suggested.

The three friends exchanged skeptical looks.

Tommy shrugged. "It's worth a shot, I guess."

Spike opened the translator function and held out her
phone, inching as close to the barricaded door as she dared.
On the other side, the dragon growled.

"Hungry, hungry, eat," the robotic voice on the phone said
a second later.

"Dragon, can you hear me?" Spike said into her phone's
speaker. The phone made a series of growls.

The dragon grumbled again. *"Prey! Eat you. Hungry!"* the
phone said.

Spike sighed, glaring at her phone. "I guess that's not
going to help."

Karim scanned the razorback entry, looking for anything
that would help them. "When razorbacks start hunting you,
they ignite their flame sacs. They keep chasing until you're
dinner or the fires are out."

"How long can that take?" Tommy asked hopefully.

Karim looked down again. "Hours," he answered.

"What if I just charge it?" Tommy asked. "We could open
the door and throw the water at it, maybe shut down its
flame sac if I get a good shot."

"It would be one of us jumping through an open door that it's already attacking," Spike said. "There's no way we would get that lucky. You'd get fried and then it would come in for us. We need more info. What else do we know about them?"

Karim glanced through the entry in Monsterpedia. "They are proud, territorial . . . they have a strong sense of honor, they won't let anyone ride on their back . . . and when they're hungry, they're vicious. That's the side we're seeing now."

"That doesn't help us much," Tommy said, frowning.

Karim shook his head. He couldn't figure it out. These rules were too restrictive. There weren't enough options to put together a plan that could beat the razorback.

Well . . . what did you do when you couldn't beat the rules? You changed the rules.

He looked around the room another time, trying to broaden his vision. How could he change the rules of the situation?

"These walls," Karim said, eyeing them speculatively. "This one is concrete." He patted the wall that held the door. "But the others . . . they're just drywall."

"Okay," Spike said. "So?"

Karim held out Sidesplitter. "This sword probably can't cut through a fire door like the one on the stairs, but *this* wall . . ." He looked over at his bulky friend. "Tommy smash?"

A grin spread over Tommy's face as he realized what was being asked of him. He took the sword and sized up the wall. "It's not smashing, exactly. Let's call it . . . remodeling."

"Remodeling?" Spike quietly pulled up her phone, flicking

the video on. Karim smiled. If they survived, this could be a pretty great moment.

"This basement has potential, but it's a real fixer-upper," Tommy said, stepping to the wall and pulling the sword back. "We're just going to take out"—he paused as he took a chop at the drywall—"this wall." He struck it a few more times. "It's just constricting the whole vibe in here," he added, then kicked the piece of drywall, forcing it to buckle inward. With a few more slices and a firm shove, Tommy staggered through the wall in a cloud of dust, revealing a hole. "See, it really opens the space up and lets it breathe."

As the drywall pieces fell to the ground, the trio heard a sharp crack behind them. Karim glanced at the door, where the dragon's nose was poking through.

"Go, go!" Spike said.

They rushed through the opening in the wall and into the corridor beyond as a blast of flame erupted from the beast's mouth.

Karim looked left and right. Two identical corridors. Neither held a path out of danger. No easy answers there. Wherever they went, the dragon could follow them. And none of them would take them to a route out.

"Where to?" Tommy asked.

"Uh . . . left," Karim said, picking at random. They ran down the corridor, putting some distance between themselves and the dragon.

"Okay, so we are slightly less trapped," Spike said as they reached the far side of the floor. "But still very trapped. We need a plan. What's our next move? Is there some way that we can still get that water down its throat?"

Karim nodded, trying to keep the flow of ideas in his head from shutting down completely as the door behind them started to crack.

"Well . . . we know that the razorback is attracted to smell," he said. "If we're going to get the water down its throat, we need to distract it."

Spike looked at Tommy, grinning widely.

"What, you're going to use me as bait?!" Tommy was furious. "No way!"

"Not you," Spike said. "Just your scent."

Karim felt himself smile as he realized what she meant. The BroteinCon ("Get so fit you don't fit in your clothes") T-shirt that Tommy was wearing was not just sweaty—around the armpits, the sweat was practically dripping off it.

"You guys just want to see me flex my glorious pecs," Tommy said after they had explained the plan to him. "Well, here you go. Gun show, tickets for two." Tommy pulled the shirt over his head and handed it to Spike.

"Gross." She wrinkled her nose and held it between two fingers as far from her as she could. "Well, let's get this over with as soon as possible."

After the heat of being trapped in that room, the cool air felt good across Tommy's back as they ran. He would probably be cold soon, but it was better than being fast-roasted barbecue dinner for a dragon.

The jug of water was feeling heavier the longer Tommy carried it, but he could handle it. This was what he'd been training for. His heart was fluttering like the wings of a hummingbird, but he set his shoulders and paid attention to what his friends were saying.

Spike and Karim had been throwing ideas back and forth the entire time they were running, in their usual shorthand of half sentences and references to things that Tommy didn't know. But Tommy didn't mind; they would let him know what he needed to do when the time came. And he was confident it would work. Pretty confident, anyway.

On the other side of the basement, they checked that the

other stairwell was definitely blocked off with one of those steel fire doors.

"As we expected," Spike said.

"I still kind of hoped," Karim said with a sigh.

"Okay, anyway, this is stage one of the plan," Spike explained. "Put out the razorback's fire so that it calms down. Then hopefully we can sneak out and find a way out of here."

"Maybe climb the elevator shaft," Karim suggested. "Or the air ducts."

"Can we really climb through air ducts?" Tommy asked, excited. He'd always wanted to do that.

"Almost certainly not," Spike said. "At least, not the way it works in movies and video games. "If it *is* possible, we'll have to cut out a way through with the sword. I *might* be able to slip through and come back and unlock the doors."

Tommy scowled. Reality was constantly ruining his fun.

"Anyway," Karim continued, "the first step is to get this dragon off our backs. According to Monsterpedia, if you can put out its flame, it'll usually run and hide while it replenishes."

Tommy was sometimes tempted to read up on all the monsters, but then Karim wouldn't get to play the role of Mr. Know-It-All. And that would be mean.

Karim used the magical sword to cut the top off the jug so that Tommy could easily throw the water in one big splash. Karim had the sweaty shirt on the end of a rope and was going to use that to draw in the razorback. When the dragon finally caught up and was able to eat the shirt, Tommy was supposed to throw the water down its throat.

"There will be a moment when the razorback grabs the shirt," Karim explained. "It will toss its head back and wolf it down. That's when you go. After that, we'll both run into this room. Spike will slam the door shut as soon as you're in."

Spike always seemed to arrange plans so that he and Karim were the ones to take the risks, but Tommy was okay with that. Karim was barely any better, though he was starting to show some spunk. But Tommy—he was born to take risks. Tommy was the bait *and* the trap.

Still, he hated to admit it, but he was kind of scared. This dragon's teeth looked *nasty*.

At first everything went smoothly. Tommy pressed up against the corner at the end of the hallway with his water, listening to the slithering sound of the approaching beast. Karim was waiting on the opposite corner, peering around the wall and slowly pulling on the rope, drawing the dragon toward them.

Tommy could see the tension in the boy's tight features and wide eyes, but he seemed to be keeping it together. The dragon advanced steadily, and Tommy's grip on the water jug tightened.

Finally, the sweaty shirt squished to a halt only a few feet away from them. Only the "Bro" in the Brotein ("Don't roll with the punches—*be* the punches") logo was visible.

Karim nodded, then dropped the rope. Tommy peeked around the corner and saw the dragon lean down and sniff.

It licked the shirt cautiously. Karim looked to be holding back from hurling. Tommy grinned. Mom and all his friends were wrong. Not *every*one hated the way he smelled after a workout.

Finally, the scaled head grabbed the shirt in its jaws and reared back to swallow it whole. This was his moment. It was time for the big play.

Tommy charged around the corner, playing what this scene would look like on a highlight reel in his head. He stepped forward as the razorback wriggled its body and neck to get the shirt to go down. Tommy raised the jug above his head, surprised by how high he had to go. Just another foot and he could—

Suddenly, the dragon spun, and for an instant Tommy made eye contact with it. Its eyes were pure red, filled with the rage of a beast on the hunt. He leaped forward with his jug, ready to deliver it into the monster's gaping jaws. But its tail whipped around as it spun, causing Tommy's legs to lift out from under him, and he tumbled backward. The jug and its water went flying, and Tommy landed hard on his back, the breath knocked from his lungs.

They never should have been here. His dad was right. How had Karim let this happen? This was no Level 1 or 2 monster, where the worst that could really happen was a broken bone or waiting a couple weeks for petrification to wear off. This was a Level 7 beast, deadly to all but the most skilled and experienced adventurers. Even the Fang in his day would have rounded up a party of four or five to take one down.

Tommy gasped for air and feebly attempted to scramble backward as the dragon scraped forward across the concrete floor. Karim shook his head, watching in frozen horror. Tommy was about to die, and he and Spike would be next.

Time seemed to stand still as the dragon advanced on his friend. Could Karim fight it? He still had Sidesplitter in his left hand, purple nail polish glimmering in the flashlight's illumination. That was what he was supposed to do now, right? The plan had failed and Tommy was about to die, so Karim was meant to charge in and save the day, using his magical sword to battle the creature. He would somehow overcome the odds. And he knew the odds of a kid going toe-to-toe with an enraged Saskatchewan razorback without a way to extinguish its flame. The enchanted sword might be able to penetrate its scales, but Karim knew he would be torn apart before he got in more than a blow or two. And with his strength, he doubted he could do more than just chip the dragon's armor, anyway.

Karim's muscles were stuck. He tried to move, but his body just wouldn't respond. *Don't do it*, every part of his body and mind were saying.

The razorback's massive bulk glimmered in the glow of the flashlight that Tommy had dropped, which was now slowly rolling down the hall and casting wild shadows as it moved. The scaled creature reared back, its flame sac filling as it prepared to turn Tommy into a charbroiled steak.

And then a thought struck Karim. He didn't have to kill the beast. That instinct—that voice telling him not to do it. That was just the fear talking. Karim was in charge here, not the fear.

He charged forward. The flame sac under the dragon's chin filled more and more, glowing orange through the thinner scaling protecting it.

Karim held the sword with both hands and lunged forward. The tip of the sword pierced the sac, and a gout of flame exploded from it. The razorback howled, and Karim leaped backward as the dragon swung its head from side to side, bursts of fire sputtering from the wound in its throat.

Karim rushed to Tommy and grabbed his hand, straining as he helped the larger boy stand. Behind them, the razorback was roaring and thrashing. Stray flames lashed across Karim's back, and he screamed as he felt blisters forming in a vicious line across his shoulders.

Ignoring the pain, he let Tommy lean on him as the two boys stumbled down the hall and into the room where Spike was waiting. She slammed the door shut behind them.

Tommy collapsed in a heap, drawing ragged and uneven breaths. Karim leaned against the wall, gritting his teeth as he felt the skin on his back change from searing pain to more of a steady throbbing.

"Took you long enough," Spike said as she locked the door. "Can you boys get anything right?" She held up her phone.

"I hope you caught all that on camera," Tommy said through ragged breaths. "That. Was. Unbelievable!"

He was right about one thing, at least: Karim was still having a hard time believing that any of that had happened.

CHAPTER 40

SPIKE

Spike jumped as something struck the door. Their plan had worked. Karim's back would have some nasty blisters, sure, but the three of them were basically intact. But this was just step one—the first of many steps that would get them out of here alive. Hopefully. And then . . . she wasn't sure what then. Still, one way or another, Mike Tuckerville was going to pay for this.

"What do we do now?" Karim asked, still wincing as he peeled off his shirt and ripped it down the middle to stretch it out so that he could tie it like a bandage over his back.

One thing was for sure: Spike was *not* going to lose any of her clothes down here. Shopping for new ones with her mom was a battle to keep from looking like an Easter egg. Spike liked her plain black T-shirts just fine, thank you very much. And that went double when they were all pulling out their phones to record every important moment for their stream, whether their faces were blurred or not.

"So what now?" Tommy asked as he finished tying the burned shirt around Karim's torso. "More remodeling?"

Outside, the razorback was scratching at the door, but the urgency of its pursuit seemed to be gone, and there was no heat from its flaming breath. The room shook slightly as a deep rumbling came from outside.

Spike pointed to the air vent in the ceiling. "It's worth a shot. If we can cut our way through to the floor above and one of us can slip through to the next floor, then they can come down and open one of the doors from the other side."

Karim nodded. "Right. We don't need to run all over the building. We just need to go up to the floor above."

A minute later they had stacked several boxes, and Tommy held them in place while Karim helped Spike climb on top. Spike peered up into the vent. She had just started unscrewing the vent's cover when she noticed something dripping from it. She turned on her phone's flashlight, then leaned out of the way as more of the green slime dripped through, almost as if reacting to her presence.

She tried to climb down but tripped, and she would have fallen hard on the concrete if her friends hadn't grabbed her arms and helped her land with some dignity.

"What is it?" Tommy asked, but Karim was already examining the slime dripping onto the box.

"It's sour ooze," Karim said. "I guess we're not getting out through the vents."

Spike had heard about this nasty creature. In confined spaces, sour ooze was an adventurer's worse nightmare. It was attracted to the heat of living things, and its acid touch would burn you up. It could make its way through tiny cracks in doors, and if you sliced it with a sword, it would just glop back together and keep coming.

The green slime oozed its way along the floor, digesting everything it came into contact with.

"Sour ooze is common in abandoned underground areas," Karim said. "A few would-be adventurers' bodies found in an old basement killed by ooze . . ."

"No one will ask too many questions," Spike finished, a grim smile on her face. "But that's not going to happen. Do they really think we're going to make it so easy?"

Suddenly, a phone in the room rang.

Karim answered the phone and put it on speaker. If someone had something to say, he wanted them all to hear it.

"What do you want now, Luis?" Spike yelled behind him. "I told you to leave us alone. But you never listen to what I say at all, do you?"

Karim sighed. This was the angriest he'd ever seen her. She'd better not ruin their chances of getting out of this mess alive. Between the razorback and the ooze, he was pretty sure they were out of options. Maybe surrendering wouldn't be the worst thing. Live on to adventure another day, right?

"Spike, I—I'm sorry," her father said through the speaker. "I'm so sorry. I tried, I really did."

"Should we maybe be a little nicer?" Karim whispered. "Do we really have any way to get out of here?"

Spike stared daggers at him. Or maybe it was more like she was staring swords at him, or ballista bolts. But Tommy was nodding sadly.

Just then, another voice—a familiar voice—came from the speaker. "Put him back in the limo, and make sure he doesn't contact anyone," the sneering voice said. "We can't have him squealing to the police, now can we?"

Karim winced as they heard what sounded like Spike's dad yelping in pain.

The smarmy voice came directly over the speaker. "This is

Mike Tuckerville," it said. "And don't worry, about how *nice* you're being. It's too late now. I'm just calling to tell you that I've released the sour ooze. I wanted you to know before you die that you've lost. I gave you an option to surrender, and I never give second chances."

"Never!" Tommy yelled. Karim wanted to beg for their lives, but instead he stayed quiet as Tommy and Spike shouted at the microphone. Karim glanced down at Tommy's phone, which was still on, still recording. At least they had that.

"Goodbye, former AppVenturers," Mike Tuckerville said. He laughed for a moment before the phone clicked and the line went dead.

Karim picked up the phone again, but there was nothing. He shook his head. "No dial tone. They've blocked it for outgoing calls."

"Okay," Tommy said. "So, uh, what do we do now?"

They stood in silence. Outside, the razorback was pacing back and forth, occasionally scratching at the door with its claws.

Karim's mind was working overtime. They could certainly bust through more of the interior walls and escape that way, but he hesitated. The dragon would just pursue them. Even without its fire, it was still more than a match for the trio.

"The razorback is still in hunting mode, even if it has calmed down. We need to buy more time," Spike said. "We can't figure out a way up the elevator if it keeps after us."

"According to Monsterpedia it should be running off to its lair to recharge," Karim said through gritted teeth. "Why hasn't it? If only we could talk to it . . ."

Spike grinned. There Karim went again, almost having the perfect idea but not quite following it through. She pulled out her phone, and in a moment Mortimer's Monsterpedia's Monster Tongue Translator was working. The dragon was no longer in full rage mode, so maybe this was worth another shot.

The razorback's claws scratched against the door and it rumbled.

"Rage. Fury. Taken from my forests," the computerized voice translated. *"Why have the giant rodents done this to me? They must suffer."*

Spike forced herself to advance to the door, holding the speaker of her phone up to the doorjamb and cranking up the volume.

"We didn't bring you here," she said into the phone's mic. "It was the other humans, the bad ones." A second later, the phone translated her words into a series of growls and roars.

"And we aren't giant rodents!" Tommy added from behind her. She shot a glance at him, but he just pouted.

The phone speaker rumbled and hissed. She was suddenly very grateful that she had opted for the newest one with the micro subwoofer.

The dragon rumbled, and the phone translated.

"You are no different from them! You have hurt me! The hurting will be for weeks, with no fire mouth. You are all the same—nothing but rodents and prey, unwilling to face me directly!"

"We only did it because you were chasing us," Spike answered. "Can you understand that? We didn't want to hurt you."

The razorback didn't respond. It shuffled its weight outside.

"Where did they take you from?" Karim asked.

Spike nodded. If they could keep it talking, then they might figure out how to persuade it to spare them.

"The mighty plateaus," the dragon answered. *"The ice and wind that have been our home since the mice with hands began to build their rock houses in the plains below."*

"Hey! We're not mice—" Tommy began, but Spike stepped on his foot. She was not going to let his pride ruin this. They had the beast talking; they could make this negotiation work.

"The same people who kidnapped you and trapped you down here have done the same to us," Spike said. "They want you to kill us."

The razorback huffed. It sounded to her like the dragon was trying to breathe fire, but all that came out was a stench that smelled like weeks-old laundry from the boys' locker room.

"And why should I believe you, Rats That Stand on Their Hind Legs?"

Behind her, Spike heard Tommy draw in his breath to object, but then huffed and walked away.

"They're releasing sour ooze into the basement," Karim said.

The dragon snorted. *"I have seen the green goo. Your hamster hides will be easy prey, but I think I will not go down so easily."*

"Your scales will protect you longer than our skin, that's true," Karim said. "But even with your strength, the ooze will eat through you just the same eventually."

"Is that true?" Spike whispered.

Karim shrugged. "Probably. Mortimer's isn't that specific. But sour ooze can eat through steel given enough time . . ."

Spike nodded, impressed. This was a different, more determined Karim than the timid boy from even just a few weeks ago.

"Even if I believed you, Gerbils That Use Tools, why should I not eat you? I have been trapped down here for days with nothing to eat."

Spike grinned. This was working. Now they were negotiating. "We can help you get out," she offered. "We can help you get home, back to your, um, your—"

"Your mighty plateaus," Karim filled in.

After a pause for the translation, the floor shook as the razorback roared, some primal mixture of laughter and rage.

"Don't lie to me, prey. You are just as trapped as I am and trying to buy yourselves a few more seconds in your brief chipmunk life spans."

Spike sighed. If this beast just didn't want to work with them, what could they do?

Tommy had returned and was hefting the magical sword. "I can take that punk," he whispered. "We hurt him once. A few bashes in the face and maybe he'll change his tune."

"No," Karim said. "Not yet. Let me try one more thing. If it goes badly, then you can charge in with the sword."

"What are you going to do?" Spike asked.

"Easy," Karim said unconvincingly. "Show it that we're not prey."

Things were happening awfully fast, and Tommy wasn't sure what needed to be punched to make the situation better. But he was ready to give this a shot.

This time it was Tommy who hid behind the wall holding Sidesplitter, while Karim stood in the open. The sword felt cold and heavy in Tommy's hands, and the chilly basement air was starting to make his bare back tingle. But if Karim's negotiation didn't work, he was more than ready to go in. All he needed was one lucky thrust.

Karim flung open the door. The razorback snorted in surprise, then advanced.

Tommy's blood ran even colder. The dragon's scales were thick and gleamed in the light from Spike's flashlight, and its jaws held rows of knife-sharp teeth. It was huge, barely able to fit through the doorframe.

The razorback stepped toward Karim. Tommy could see his friend shaking, and yet the boy gave no ground. Finally, the razorback stopped only a foot from Karim, their faces at the same level, one scaled and horned, the other a smooth human face set in determination.

"We're both stuck down here," Karim said, looking the beast in the eye. "Give us half an hour to figure out how to escape. If we can't do it, then we'll still be here. And we can fight it out then."

Spike didn't look happy to be this close to such a creature at all, but she stood only a few feet away and held the phone up so that its translation could be heard.

"Hungry. Trapped for days. My flames cannot burn through the silver doors. Must . . . eat one of you. Will help other two," the dragon said.

There was a long silence as the trio exchanged nervous looks.

"So . . . do we draw straws, rock-paper-scissors—how do you want to handle this?" Spike asked. It sounded like a joke, but Tommy wasn't quite sure.

"Um, maybe it doesn't need to eat a person. Do we have any food?" Karim asked. "All I brought was a water bottle."

Tommy stood up straight. Now *this*—this was a problem that Tommy Wainwright could handle. "I've got you, Mr. Dragon," he said.

He unwrapped three of his Brotein ("Never put off lifting until tomorrow that which you can lift today") bars and tossed them on the ground in front of the razorback.

In an instant, its jaws jerked out and consumed all the bars in toothy mouthfuls. It glared at him, and Tommy sighed.

Tommy tossed it the two backup bars that he kept in the small outside pouch. The beast ate those just as quickly, then looked at Tommy, opened its mouth slightly, and growled.

"Oh, *fine*," Tommy said, throwing in the final bar from the very bottom of his backpack. And then the half-eaten bar in his front pocket, just in case. "But you owe me!"

He had only one left now, broken in half and hidden in his back pocket. It was salt and vinegar, his favorite. Other protein bars had flavors like chocolate or blueberry. The folks who made Brotein ("Might not make right, but it sure makes awesome") weren't afraid to take risks with flavor.

After eating, the dragon roared again, this time sounding more like a laugh. *"You have until this pain in my flame sac becomes unbearable, and I lose control,"* it said. *"Make the time count, Lemmings That Smell of Tomatoes, Cheese, and Grease."*

As the razorback turned and shuffled away down the hall, Spike snorted. "He has a point about that one," she said, rolling her eyes at Tommy.

Tommy ignored her and stood up straight. If he smelled like those things, then so be it. He'd rather die smelling of pizza than live not eating pizza.

As they walked out of the room, Karim drew in a sharp breath. "Look," he said, pointing his flashlight at the door.

The bluish glow illuminated one of the locked doors keeping them trapped. At the bottom, ooze was glittering in the light as it seeped into the subbasement.

"Well, there goes that option," Spike said with a groan.

"We are so screwed," Karim said. "We are so, *so* screwed."

Tommy shook his head. This wouldn't do. He didn't know the way out, but he knew that Karim and Spike could come up with something.

"I'm not giving up yet," Tommy said, trying to put confidence in his voice that he didn't feel. "What do you always say, Spike? You're not allowed to give up until you've tried all the options."

"Yeah, yeah, you're right," Spike said. "Let's go check out the elevators."

A minute later they inspected the elevators with their flashlights. There were three in a row, right in the middle of the basement. Their metal doors shone in the light.

"All we need to do is get in there and climb up, right?" Tommy said, feeling hope starting to grow inside him. "You guys solved it again!"

Tommy pressed the button, but of course nothing happened. He tried to grab the doors and force them open, but every time he pulled, his fingers couldn't get enough of a hold to pull them apart. He tried the other two doors, but they were no better than the first.

"We'll need a crowbar or something to get these open," Spike said. "Did we see anything like that in any of those rooms? Office basements have useful stuff like that in them, right?"

Tommy swept his flashlight over the hallways around them. He could see the sour ooze advancing at the edge of each hallway. "Even if there is, we don't have much time. That ooze is getting close!"

Karim shrugged. "Maybe it's time to once again use my father's magical sword for something completely different than what it was intended."

He stepped to the door and used the sword's supernaturally sharp point to wedge the blade between the elevator doors. He gestured to Tommy, who felt himself grinning.

"Okay, doors," Tommy said, cracking his knuckles, "time for round two." Tommy heaved on the sword, and after a moment felt the doors starting to budge. Quickly, Spike and Karim each grabbed one of the doors and pulled with all their might.

With a grinding, the doors inched farther and farther apart, until finally there was enough room for them to fit through. Tommy leaned in to have a look, running his flashlight up and down the empty shaft. Suddenly, he pulled back with a yelp.

On every surface of the elevator shaft, sour ooze was seeping in from the outside.

"They've got us," Karim said, and he knew it was true.

"It seems like they know exactly what we're doing," Spike added, "and can counter everything we try."

Karim looked around, searching with his flashlight.

"What are you looking for?" Tommy asked.

"If I were an evil mastermind like Tuckerville, I would want to know what was going on down here," Karim said. "Ah, there it is!"

In the corner, Karim found a tiny hidden camera.

Karim frowned, then took Sidesplitter from Tommy and stepped up to the camera. Okay, one stab from the sword, and . . . okay, two stabs from the sword, and . . .

"Let me do it." Tommy took the sword and, using his brute strength and height, smashed the camera's lens.

They quickly checked the immediate area, breaking two more cameras, and returned to the elevators. Karim surveyed the floor with his flashlight. The sour ooze was coming even closer.

"So," Spike said, "current situation: The ooze will get to us in a few minutes. We have an open elevator shaft, but we have to climb up the shaft without touching anything."

Karim tried to quiet the wild, nervous fluttering in his stomach and focus on the problem. But they were just so, so screwed.

"Could we put something on our hands to protect them?" he suggested.

Karim ripped a piece of his shirt and dipped it into the closest blob of sour ooze. The part that touched the ooze melted away like paper caught on fire.

"Even if we could climb with stuff on our hands," Spike announced, "it looks like the ooze eats through things too fast."

Tommy flopped to the ground, leaning his sweaty back against the wall. "Any more ideas, geniuses?" he asked. "I don't want to die like this! Not eaten by sour ooze. I always wanted to die in an epic battle defending a castle against a horde of evil monsters!"

"I always wanted to die from eating too much tapioca pudding," Spike said. "Karim, what about you?"

Karim sighed. Tommy had a point. Both of their plans had come to nothing.

The ground shook slightly as heavy footsteps approached. Karim flinched as he felt warm breath on the back of his neck. He spun to see the razorback eyeing the open elevator shaft.

"The way is open," the app translated.

"I don't want to die," Karim said. But he took one look at the dragon, and a plan started to form. "And I don't think I'm going to. Take us with you, dragon."

The razorback eyed him skeptically. Karim swallowed hard, seeing its rows of teeth as it worked its jaw.

"Just let us ride up the elevator shaft," Karim said. "That's it."

"Honor commands that I repay you for your assistance in opening the door," the razorback replied. *"But honor also demands that I not allow you to ride on my back. I'm sorry, but I will not. I thank you for your help all the same."*

The dragon started toward the elevator shaft, and Karim took a deep breath. He had to act now, or it would be too late, and they would die down here, forgotten.

He stepped forward, putting himself in the elevator door, squarely between the razorback and the escape route.

"No," he said. "Take us with you."

The razorback opened its mouth and roared. *"Remove yourself!"*

Karim stared into the face of death. It was scaled, dark eyed, full of teeth, and surrounded by vicious talons. Karim's whole body was shaking, and every instinct said to flee. Every strand of his human DNA told him that this beast was far too large and far too dangerous to face.

But Karim didn't move. For once, the fear shut up. "Take us with you, or kill me," Karim finally said, and he heard rustling as Tommy and Spike stepped to his side.

The razorback glared at them. It roared again, but they withstood the force of its damp breath. Long seconds passed as the standoff continued. Behind the razorback, Karim could see the sour ooze approaching, sliming its way along the floor and walls.

Just then, one of the other elevator shafts rumbled to life.

They all froze, even the dragon. What fresh madness was this? Spike shook her head. Weren't a locked basement, sour ooze, and a real dragon enough?

With the one shaft open, they could hear the elevator moving downward, and even see the car as it pulled up from the floor below in the next shaft.

"What's happening?" Karim asked.

"Is someone coming to help us?" Tommy added.

"Maybe it's monster control?" Karim offered, a note of desperate hope in his voice.

Spike shook her head. Somehow she knew it wouldn't be that. Mike Tuckerville wanted them dead. Of course he had some fresh trick up his sleeve.

She paused for a moment, listening. There was movement in the elevator. Something, or somethings, jumping around. They sounded far too small and far too hyperactive to be human.

"It isn't monster control," Spike said. "It's more monsters."

The elevator gave a ding. Next to her, Tommy hefted Sidesplitter.

The door opened, and for a moment there was silence in the basement. And then a shrieking horde of small bodies piled out of the elevator.

"Gremlins!" Spike said with distaste.

The gremlins' faces were distorted in rage.

"They look angry," Tommy said.

"Hungry," Karim added.

"Tuckerville probably left them trapped in there for a day or more," Spike said.

The gremlins hissed, and one in the lead bared its teeth. Spike could see a very faint bruise in the face of the lead gremlin. Was this the same gremlin that Spike had knocked out with her ring? It was hard to tell for sure, and it got even harder as the gremlins charged.

Tommy stepped forward, swinging the sword in a wide arc. The gremlins leaped back, frightened of the enchanted blade. But a moment later they began creeping forward again.

"Hold them back," Spike said, turning to the dragon.

"I can't do this for long!" Tommy said, pointing the sword at an advancing gremlin. "There are way too many of them."

Just then, a ding and a squelching sound echoed from the third elevator shaft. Spike spun to see a tentacle coming out of the opening elevator door. She shouted, but before anyone could react, one of the blue tentacles had wrapped around Karim's leg.

With a yelp, the boy fell to the ground. He flailed about and grabbed the frame of the open shaft.

Spike reacted immediately, jumping to Karim's aid. She grabbed him under the arms and braced herself against the doorframe, helping to hold him in place as the tentacles reached from the darkness of the other elevator and took hold of his legs.

"Can you kick it off?" she asked.

"It's too tight!" Karim answered.

Spike felt Karim slipping away, inch by inch. She gritted her teeth and pulled. At first her feet slipped, but then she found a grip on the doorframe and wrapped her leg around it. A bit of sour ooze began to eat at one of her shoes, but she ignored it.

She wasn't going to let Tuckerville win this one. She dug in and reached a standstill.

"What is that thing?" Tommy asked as he continued to hold back the menacing gremlins with wide sweeps of the sword.

"A pit lurker!" Karim shouted.

Spike was straining to hold Karim in place. "How do we beat it?"

"You're not going to like this, but . . . I need to look it up. Hold on!" Karim said.

"What? Okay, I guess." Spike gripped Karim, holding him in place.

He was grasping the doorframe with one hand, phone in the other, and skimming the entry on pit lurkers.

PIT LURKER

LEVEL 5 MONSTER

The pit lurker is exactly what it sounds like. Deep in the recesses of a cave, it lies in wait for unsuspecting adventurers. Then its blue tentacles shoot out and grapple them, pulling them down to a squishy grave.

HABITAT: Any caves in the dark and the damp can be home to pit lurkers.

THREAT ANALYSIS: Pit lurkers are deadly foes, with a multitude of incredibly strong tentacles. Once one has a grip on its prey, very little can cause it to let go. And even if you do manage to cut one with a magical weapon, there are many more waiting to take its place.

WEAKNESSES: Pit lurkers share a similar skin texture to the common snail. Especially in dry environments, pit lurkers are vulnerable to salt. In fact, they have such a strong aversion to it that a few shakes of a saltshaker is enough to give them pause.

MORTIMER'S NOTES: The original entry on these monsters said that no one had ever seen the actual face of a pit lurker and lived to tell the tale. One summer on an adventure in Egypt, I took it upon myself to change that. I succeeded, but only at the cost of a lifetime of nightmares. If you think the tentacles are gross, you do *not* want to see what I have seen.

"Salt!" Karim yelled. "We need to put salt on it!"

"Um, it's not like we brought a picnic basket down here," Spike said. "Tommy, any chance you brought a saltshaker or some salt packets or something?"

"No, sorry!" Tommy said, cutting a wide arc through the air and sending a crowd of gremlins skittering backward. "Oh, wait. I do have a salt-and-vinegar Brotein bar . . ."

"I guess that's our only chance. Where is it?" Spike said, but she could already see it peeking out the top of his back pocket. "Okay, I see it. Just . . . back up. As close to us as you can."

Tommy backed up, wielding the sword with his two hands as the gremlins started closing in.

"Ow!" Karim yelped. "It's starting to squeeze!"

Gritting her teeth, Spike reached up. It wasn't really where she wanted to be sticking her hand, but this was a desperate situation. She reached in and pulled the bar from Tommy's back pocket. With one hand still holding on, she managed to use her teeth to open the wrapper and rubbed the bar on the tentacle gripping Karim's leg.

A high-pitched whine came from the other elevator shaft, and the tentacles jerked back into the darkness.

Spike jumped and turned to the dragon, who had been watching all this without making a move. It seemed that the gremlins knew better than to attack a dragon and were focused entirely on the humans.

"Will you help us?" Spike faced the dragon and took a deep breath. "Please?"

The dragon grunted in response.

"We are trapped here by the same evil man," Spike said. "He wanted us to fight and kill each other. Help us escape, together."

"Show us what a powerful dragon you are," Karim added. "Show that you are better than—"

"Ow!" Tommy said from behind them, kicking away a gremlin that made it past him and took a bite of his leg. "They're fast little things!"

Finally, the dragon folded its legs and splayed out its wings. It rumbled quietly. Spike could hear the annoyance in that sound. She didn't need the translator to understand what the razorback was saying; she could read it in the beast's eyes. Anger, pride . . . and perhaps a grudging respect?

The dragon rumbled again. *"Climb on, then,"* the translation app said.

Karim and Spike jumped on, and Spike watched as Tommy stayed behind to provide backup support. The dragon climbed into the shaft on top of the elevator car that was parked at the floor below.

"Tommy, get on!" Spike yelled.

He gave one final broad swing of the sword, sending the gremlins jumping back one more time. He turned and leaped onto the dragon, scrambling up to its neck.

Tommy clung there, while Spike was at the dragon's tail and Karim somehow wedged between them. The gremlins had surrounded them, and he did his best to continue threatening them with the sword, but they crowded into the elevator shaft, attempting to climb on top of the dragon.

Tommy yelped as one of the gremlins jumped up and clawed at him. Their flashlights were off, so the only light available filtered down from somewhere far above. He kicked at it savagely and felt a thump as his shoe struck it in the chest and it fell back. Behind him, he could hear Spike and Karim grappling with their own gremlins.

A few times the creature's wings scraped the ooze on the walls, and a sizzling sound filled the air. As its wings flexed in the wide elevator shaft, Tommy suddenly had the sense of this creature's immense size. In the basement, it had been huge, even folded in on itself.

A gremlin somehow jumped past Tommy's guard and sank its teeth into his left leg. He grabbed it and pulled, while still trying to keep the sword in action, but its teeth were locked on him.

Suddenly, the dragon's powerful legs flexed, and it leaped upward. For a moment, everything lurched. In the darkness, Tommy couldn't quite understand what was happening. There was the rush of air around him as the powerful wings flapped, and the dragon appeared to be using its claws to push off the walls, as if running up the shaft, picking up speed to take flight.

The last thing he saw from the basement was a glimpse of the gremlins pouncing on the remaining Brotein ("Knowledge is power—but so are muscles") bar that was lying on the floor. What a terrible waste. Even though it was probably covered in tentacle slime, he still kind of wished Spike had managed to grab it. You never knew when you would be *really* hungry. Was there a five-second rule for tentacle slime?

The gremlin loosened its grip for a moment, and Tommy yanked, pulling the thing off his leg. As the dragon began to ascend, he tossed it to the ground. One of the flashlights illuminated it for a moment, hissing and gesturing rudely at him from the ground below. He glanced back to see Karim and Spike were both holding on, and seemed to have survived the gremlin onslaught.

Tommy heard the sizzling of armored claws meeting sour ooze as the razorback struggled to gain altitude. Gremlins kept jumping at them, but with three humans kicking and Tommy's sword poking at them, the last ones fell off as the dragon ascended the first two stories.

For the next few seconds there was only the scraping of claw against concrete, the flapping of wings, and the rumblings of the dragon. Through the scales, Tommy could feel its massive muscles flexing, working hard in the confined space.

With the lurching movement and the rushing air, Tommy was forced to close his eyes. Some wild combination of wings, claws, and sheer force of dragon will propelled them upward. He knew that the bite on his leg would hurt later, but for now all he could focus on was holding on to the dragon's neck.

Tommy clung to the creature, feeling his fingers scrape against its armorlike scales. Karim's grasp on Tommy's leg was like a vise, almost cutting off his circulation. Tommy felt his grip slip on the rough scales, but with a wild lunge he grabbed hold again. He clenched harder and managed to stay on. He hadn't been exercising every day with the Gripmaster 2000 to have his hands fail him now. He was Tommy. He was strength and power. And he would hold on!

At last, the wild swaying stopped. In the darkness, Tommy could hear only panting for long seconds, some from the humans and the loudest by far from a powerful dragon throat.

Spike's light flicked on. They were perched near the top of the shaft, the dragon straddling its legs wide to hold them in place.

The dragon rumbled and poked its head against one of the elevator doors, but no one had the translation app running. Still, they understood well enough.

Balancing precariously on the dragon, this was twice as hard as it had been down below. Karim and Spike helped to brace Tommy as he slid Sidesplitter's tip in between the elevator doors.

Tommy roared. Some jobs required clever and oddball ideas, like the ones Karim had. Some took strategy and a ruthless determination to win. That was Spike. And some took guts and raw strength. That was Tommy.

He strained against the door, the pain in his cut-up hands flaring. But that was nothing. Pain was the feeling of victory coming closer. He heaved, and the doors slid open. Once they were parted enough for the dragon to put its head through, Tommy pulled the sword, handed it off to Karim to sheathe, and let the beast force the doors open with its powerful neck. Tommy closed his eyes and hung on tight as the dragon pushed its way through the door and carried them out of the elevator.

Tommy had thought that the dragon would stop to let them off, but it kept its momentum and strode forward. They were in a large office space at the very top of the eight-story building, and moonlight was streaming in through large floor-to-ceiling windows that circled them.

"Oh no," Karim said. "No, no, no."

"Everyone hold on!" Spike advised.

The dragon lumbered forward, and Tommy realized

almost too late what was about to happen. He closed his eyes and ducked his head close to the razorback's neck. The dragon roared as glass shattered around them and it leaped out into the sky.

For a moment they plummeted, and Tommy had a vision of three kids and a dragon, all splattered on the street below. Then, with a great *whoosh*, the wings flapped, and Tommy was suddenly weightless.

This wasn't like the lurching, blind madness of the elevator shaft. Tommy was flying. It was like nothing he had ever experienced before. The rush of the air around him, the buildings zipping by below. With every beat of the dragon's wings, Tommy's heart nearly stopped. But when the dragon started to glide, Tommy's cut-up hands and Karim's vise grip on his leg were completely forgotten.

They were out.

47 SPIKE

The dragon set the trio down in a park a couple blocks from the office building. All three of them tumbled off and lay on the ground.

Flying had been amazing, but the whole experience left Spike woozy. She tried to stand up, but felt a wave of dizziness and knelt back down on the ground and gasped.

"How does it fly like that?" Spike whispered. "It must weigh a couple tons! Those wings aren't that big." It just didn't make sense that a hunk of bones and scales that heavy could possibly become airborne.

"Thaumatologists speculate that it has some way of counteracting gravity," Karim explained, trying to remember the article that he'd read on this last year. "But no one really knows. Aeronautical engineers say that it just doesn't make sense."

"Do not let appearances deceive you," the dragon said, a

voice rumbling from its throat rather than the app. "I
am . . . very aerodynamic."

"You . . . you speak English! Why didn't you tell us?" Spike
demanded. Was this thing serious? Had it really been able to
speak and understand them all this time? She wanted
to wring its neck but realized that trying to do so would
probably hurt her hands.

"You never asked me, did you?" the razorback answered,
laughter rumbling in its belly. "You just assumed."

"That's crazy!" Tommy complained. "How should we have
known to ask?"

"I suppose that I would not have told you, anyway," the dragon
said. "True dragon kin speak all languages. But it is a great
honor for me to speak to you in your language. Earlier, you
had not yet earned it. Now you have saved me and I have saved
you. We are bonded. You are quite clever gerbils. I thank you."

Tommy and Karim seemed to be looking at the razorback
with awe and reverence, but Spike scoffed. All this honor
junk was the sort of thing that got you killed. If she hadn't
had the translation app ready to go, they all would have died
in that basement. All because this overgrown salamander
apparently had an ego the size of Montana.

"Do you have a name?" Karim asked.

"I do," the razorback answered. "Among my people, I am
called Pipsqueak."

Spike couldn't help but laugh and heard the others trying
to hide their amusement.

The dragon looked at them with what seemed clearly to be a scowl. "A dragon does not choose their own name," Pipsqueak said. "And I am the smallest of my clan. But one day, I will be queen. Size matters not, when you have spirit."

Spike grinned at that, and for a moment it seemed the dragon inclined her head in acknowledgment.

Pipsqueak turned to leave.

"Wait!" Tommy said, stepping forward. "I have one more question for you. Why do you keep calling us rodents?"

The razorback looked down at Tommy, her bulk making even his size seem insignificant. "It is the correct name, of course. You have your categories for things, and so do we. The razorbacks group animals together by taste," Pipsqueak explained. "Rodents are the most delicious group."

"Goodbye, Gecko with Wings," Spike said, smiling sweetly at the dragon.

The dragon snorted and turned away. She took two lumbering steps, and as she accelerated, the awkward lumps of her body seemed to fall into place. As she reached a gallop, every motion was smooth, more like a cheetah than the awkward hippo that she had seemed in the elevator shaft. She stretched her wings, flapped three times as she ran, and launched into the air.

"Dragons are jerks," Tommy said.

"She's beautiful," Karim said, staring after the razorback's disappearing form as she flew, outlined against the moon. "Is this what falling in love feels like?"

Spike wondered if the whole moon outline thing was on

purpose. The razorback certainly seemed to love drama. "You spent all last year crushing on Anna Suarez, dummy."

"Yeah, but now I don't think those were real feelings," Karim said, staring wistfully into the night. "That was just dumb kid stuff."

"How exactly would that work?" Spike asked. "You dating a dragon?"

"Uh, guys?" Tommy said, and Spike brought her focus back from the creature, which was admittedly mesmerizing. "Someone's coming."

Headlights shone on them as a big black SUV approached, coming on fast. Spike blinked for a moment in the glare, then brought her own light up to shine it on the vehicle. Before they could react, the SUV had skidded to a stop. The doors sprung open, and figures piled out.

One of them she recognized immediately, with his hooded sweatshirt and a shiny, metallic green tie.

48 TOMMY

As soon as Spike pointed, Tommy recognized the figure. Mike Tuckerville. He wasn't sure how much of it was fear and how much was rage, but Tommy grinned as he felt a surge of adrenaline.

Accompanying Tuckerville was a group of people holding what looked like harpoon guns. Probably tipped with enchanted daggers—one of the few things that could penetrate dragon scales. Guns, of course, would be useless against a powerful magical beast like a razorback.

"Should we run?" Tommy asked.

"We'd never make it," Karim said, looking at the lights closing in from behind them.

"Stall him!" Spike whispered. Karim was already poking at his phone, and he and Spike seemed to have some plan in motion. Did Tommy have a clue what it was? No. Did it matter? Also no. He knew what he had to do. It was showtime.

Tommy stepped forward, waving cheerfully.

"Sorry about that, pal!" he said. "Looks like you just missed the razorback! I think she's coming back around, though. Should be here in a minute."

Tuckerville's eyes widened for a moment, but a woman wearing dark sunglasses and holding a tablet shook her head dismissively.

"Satellite says the monster is headed due north, sir," she said. "It's not a threat."

"Might I say, sir," Tommy began, "that you look fantastic in that bright green tie? It really, ahem, ties together the whole ensemble." He stepped forward and grabbed the AppVenture CEO's hand, shaking it vigorously. "And might I say that it is an absolute *honor* to meet such a distinguished entrepreneur as yourself!"

Tuckerville was staring at him in confusion, obviously not sure what to make of such friendly behavior from someone he'd just tried to kill.

"I've been a huge fan of yours ever since you made your first fortune with the Cash 4 Magic Items scam—er, I mean, totally legitimate business," Tommy continued.

Tuckerville narrowed his eyes and glared at Tommy. "What's your game, kid?"

"Just trying to be the best Independent Adventure Contractor I can be, every day, Mr. Tuckerville, sir. I say my prayers to AppVenture every night, like a good Contractor."

"Aren't you mad at me?" Tuckerville asked.

"Oh, no!" Tommy said. "I trust that everything you do is

for the best. Releasing the sour ooze into the basement was the perfect way to go after the razorback. In the end, sacrificing a few adventurers is worth all the lives you'll save taking a dangerous dragon like that off the streets."

Tuckerville just stared in confusion, but the woman in sunglasses wasn't having any of it. "Take them," she said with a sigh.

"Wait!" Tommy protested. "Don't you want to hear about the treasure map that we found down there?"

"Treasure map?" Tuckerville asked. "How is that possible? It's just an old office building!"

"No, no, it was actually built on the site of an ancient elfin home tree," Tommy said. "There were the roots of the tree and carved on one of them was a map that only I memorized. I have a photographic memory, you see. The inscription read, 'To find the ancient elfin doubloons, you must travel under the full moon—'"

"He's full of it," the woman interrupted, pointing forward. Instantly, a very large man grabbed Tommy from behind. He struggled for a moment, but the guy knew some kind of pressure point hold, and Tommy realized with a yelp that no matter how strong he was, he was only going to get himself hurt. He was going to have to learn some of those wrestling tricks at some point.

A moment later, he saw Karim and Spike pulled up behind him the same way.

"Take their phones," Tuckerville ordered. "And that junky purple sword they claim is a magical item."

They were roughly searched, and each of their phones was stabbed in turn with one of the harpoon guns. The electronics and magical spear tips did not interact nicely, leaving each of the phones a pile of rubble.

"What do we do with them now, boss?" Sunglasses asked, eyeing the three kids like they were leftovers that no one wanted to eat.

"Well, adventurers go missing all the time," Tuckerville said. "Will anyone really care about a few more?"

Sunglasses nodded. "Their parents will sue us, but we can just slow that down for years in the courts. Everyone knows adventuring is risky, and we have records of these three accepting the adventure."

"That's it exactly," Tuckerville said. "Adventuring is inherently risky. That's what it says in the warning every time you open the app. Just another few kids who bit off more than they could chew."

Tommy was ready to struggle and fight to the death, but he noticed that Spike was standing calmly, smiling at the AppVenture CEO. Karim wasn't looking quite as cocky, but he was nowhere near as panicked as he should have been.

"That all makes perfect sense," Spike said. "Too bad it would mean the end of your business and a nice long jail sentence for both of you."

"What are you talking about, girl?" Sunglasses demanded.

"While you were listening to Tommy's very convincing story," she said, winking at him, "we uploaded all our videos."

"That includes the razorback telling us that you kidnapped it, and the phone call where you said you were going to kill us," Karim said. "And it's all online right now."

"What?!" Mike Tuckerville shrieked. "Is that true?"

The woman was already on her tablet, tapping. "Hold on," she said.

Spike grinned.

"Wait, I have to log in to my account . . ."

Karim looked around nervously.

"Just loading the page now . . ."

Tuckerville stamped impatiently. "*Well?*"

"They uploaded it before we iced the phones," Sunglasses said. "It's online and trending already."

Tuckerville clenched his fists and took a step forward, rage mixing with confusion on his face. Sunglasses stopped him, shaking her head.

Karim stared, trying to make sense of it all. They had an advantage, but this wasn't over.

"If you've already screwed me over, why shouldn't we just kill you now?" Tuckerville demanded, veins standing out on his forehead.

Karim didn't want to say anything, but no one else was offering a reason. He tried to think it through as quickly as possible. They were winning, but Tuckerville was right. If Tuckerville got desperate enough, he was capable of anything.

"If we're not hurt, you can play the whole thing off as a prank," Karim said, looking the AppVenture CEO directly in the eyes. The boy's whole body was shaking, but he didn't care. "If three kids turn up missing in the same location, in the same day . . ."

Tuckerville stared him down, but Karim didn't flinch. He felt the agent's grip holding him in place start to loosen.

Spike spoke up, shaking off the man holding her. "You can keep your business and not go to jail. Or you can do something stupid. Your call, buddy."

Karim winced. Why was she antagonizing him?

Tuckerville sneered at them.

"And give us our sword back!" Tommy added.

"What, this?" Tuckerville tossed the purple-coated sword on the ground. "That's the most hideous 'magical' sword I've ever seen. Not even Cash 4 Magic Items would take that junk."

"Sir," Sunglasses said, "we should get going. Remember the long game. What we're really trying to accomplish—the reason we started AppVenture in the first place."

"Fine," Tuckerville growled, glaring at the three friends in turn. He took a moment to look at each of them, as if fixing them in his mind for a later revenge. Karim crushed away the voice screaming in his head. He was going to be strong now. There would be time to be terrified later.

Sunglasses gently pulled her boss away, and the rest of the AppVenture crew followed. The SUV's doors slammed shut, and the vehicle sped away with a squeal of tires.

And then, suddenly, a vehicle was coming from the other direction, with red-and-white lights blazing. The police car pulled a U-turn, and in the distance they saw the black SUV pulling over to the side of the road.

Karim strained his eyes, trying to see. The police were out of their car, shining bright flashlights into the windows of the AppVenture SUV.

And then there was a sight that made his heart soar. One of the police officers pushing Tuckerville against the black SUV, pulling his hands behind him, and snapping handcuffs on him.

Two more police cars pulled up, sirens on and lights ablaze.

"We need to get out of here," Spike said.

Once again, they ran. They left the park and headed down the road where they had come from. In the background they heard more police sirens, but before long the sounds were just a distant drone.

When they were too tired to run anymore, the three friends slowed down and walked along the road. Somewhere, an owl hooted. The first rays of sunlight were just starting to peek over the horizon and the early commuters were beginning to appear.

Karim laughed, staring up at the moon and letting the insanity of it all wash over him. They'd befriended a dragon, escaped a dungeon full of deadly monsters, and faced down a wealthy and powerful psychopath. *Not a bad Tuesday*, Karim thought.

Just then, Karim heard a rustling. Tommy and Spike must have heard it too because they all turned to face the nearby bushes. Karim's eyes widened as a figure stepped out of the shadows—a familiar figure he hadn't seen in quite some time.

Spike sighed and, in a dead, flat voice, said, "Hello, Luis."

"Colleen—sorry—Spike . . . are you okay?" Luis asked.

In the moonlight, his face looked drained and tight. He might not have been trapped in a deadly dungeon all night, but he clearly hadn't slept in a long time.

Spike just glared at him for a long moment. He had the nerve to show up now? After all this? She wanted to choke him. She wanted to ignore him, maybe even get him fired.

"We're fine," Karim answered when it became clear that Spike wasn't going to. "Tuckerville and his crew left us alone after we uploaded all our data."

"We beat them, Mr. Hernandez!" Tommy added. "We did it!"

"Yeah, we did," Spike said, her voice almost a hiss. "No thanks to you, Luis."

"Honey," her dad pleaded, "I had no idea what was going on. And then it was too late. I just wanted to make a deal to get you out of there."

Spike shook her head and felt the muscles in her neck

clench tightly. "Next time, don't try to do me any favors," she said. "Better yet, don't let there *be* a next time."

She wanted to punch him. She wanted to hug him. She wanted to run away.

"Okay, I understand," he said with a sigh. His shoulders were slumped. "But I've just—"

"WHAT?" Spike asked. "What did you already go and do?"

She wanted to slap him. She wanted to cry. She wanted to scream.

"I won't be going back to AppVenture," her father said quickly. "Before I hijacked the self-driving limousine, I found the data on their catch-and-release program. I'm going to share it publicly. Oh, and I also paid out all the money for your jobs that they've been holding up. We IT guys have access to pretty much all the systems."

Spike chewed her lip as she considered this. It was something. Not nearly enough, but something.

Out of the corner of her eye, she could see Tommy dancing, moving his hips in disorienting ways that Spike had never imagined, didn't want to look directly at, and hoped that she wouldn't remember.

"We're going to Adventure Camp! We're going to Adventure Camp!" Tommy sang under his breath.

Something caught in Spike's throat. Her dad was trying hard. She might hate him, but she had to recognize that he was trying.

She swallowed and blinked. They were still on an

adventure. They had a job to do. She could focus on that, and deal with whatever these feelings were later.

"Don't share it publicly," Spike told her father. "Take it straight to the Federal Monster Administration. They can protect you if Tuckerville tries to hit you back."

"Good idea," Luis said. "Will do."

"Thanks, Mr. Hernandez," Tommy said. "We know you weren't trying to kill us."

"Spike," her dad said, his voice sad and small. "I know this is a bad time to ask. But I haven't talked to you in months. I just wanted to say . . . would it be okay if I came back and visited you sometime? I'd been talking with your mother about visiting on your birthday this year . . ."

The seconds stretched into a minute as Spike stood perfectly still.

She wanted to kick him. She wanted to tell him everything about their adventures. She wanted never to speak to him again. She wanted to hug him.

"No thanks," she said.

For a moment, everyone stood in awkward silence, and Luis looked crushed.

"But . . ." Spike began, sighing. "I guess you can call me on my birthday. If you want."

Her dad took a deep breath. His eyes were sad, but he was smiling. "Okay. I'd like that. I suppose I should probably stay away from AppVenture for a while. I'm going to stay in town and see if I can talk to your mother. I've finally been sending her the money I owe, but I owe her some apologies as well."

"Sure," Spike said. "Goodbye, Dad." She turned and walked away. After a moment, she could hear her two friends following behind her.

She knew her dad was still standing there, watching them leave. Probably crying. But she didn't look back. Maybe he wasn't total trash, but she wasn't going to give him that satisfaction.

She wanted to talk to him again. At least one more time.

They walked the long distance to the bus station in silence. Though they seemed to be out of danger, Karim could still feel his heart pounding in his chest. They had been walking for about twenty minutes when an SUV pulled up beside them.

For a moment Karim thought it would be Tuckerville again, but the window rolled down and Sally "the Sheriff" Smithfield's face leered at them.

"School started an hour ago, and you don't look like you're even hurrying to get there," Ms. Smithfield said.

"Huh? How did you—" Karim started, but before he could say more, the van's doors opened and a group of grown-ups piled out. Karim's mom grabbed him in a tight hug, and he could see that Spike's mom and Tommy's dad were doing the same to their kids.

"I'm so glad you're okay!" Mrs. Wainwright said, a pleading note in her voice. "You were supposed to be home by nine—and then we heard about that building that collapsed under the weight of sour ooze—your phone signal disappeared all night, but we saw it reappear in that park for a bit and came over as fast as we could!"

"Sorry. Um . . . it's okay, Mom," Tommy said. "We're fine."

Karim could have kicked himself. When his parents got him a phone upgrade for his birthday, they had turned tracking on so they would always be able to find him.

It took all of a minute for the four parents' relief to turn into suspicion.

"Where, exactly, *were* you three miscreants?" the Sheriff demanded.

Karim knew instinctively not to give too much away. Making up stories had never been his strong suit.

Spike didn't disappoint him, and took the lead. "We heard there was some kind of monster in that building!" she said. "Then it turned out to be sour ooze, and we got trapped for a bit. But we made it out, no harm done!"

Karim nodded, impressed. Technically, she hadn't even lied.

"It's okay, as long as you're safe!" Big Tom said, clutching his son tight, tears in his eyes.

"No, it is not!" Ms. Hernandez said. Her hand was on Spike's shoulder, but it looked like Ms. Hernandez knew better than to grab Spike too tightly. "I have been worried sick all night! And your father has been calling me nonstop and was very evasive about what was going on!"

"I talked to Dad," Spike said, and Karim noticed

Ms. Hernandez's eyebrows shoot up as she realized that Spike hadn't called her dad by his first name. "We had a chat. He knows I'm okay."

That seemed to shut Ms. Hernandez up, as she considered the new state of affairs.

"Well, isn't that all just well and dandy." Ms. Smithfield pressed a button on her keychain and the minivan's doors opened up. "But the fact remains that you skipped out on school and caused a ton of worry and wasted time."

Karim, Spike, and Tommy all sighed at the same time. They knew there was no easy way of getting out of this one.

"Now, you little jailbirds get in the back, and we'll have you cleaned up and back in time for third period. I'd hate for you to miss social studies. We can handle the paperwork for your detention later, shall we say, during your lunch period?"

They all climbed into the minivan as the three kids continued to dodge questions from their parents and guidance counselor. At some point Karim would have to mention that the new cell phone his parents bought him for his birthday was now long gone, but that could wait for later. They were in enough trouble as it was.

When he got home, Karim's dad was waiting in the kitchen. He gave a sigh as Karim entered, looking at him with a wistful look.

"I know, Dad. Adventuring is too dangerous. I shouldn't have been out there." Karim hung his head. "And I should have learned from you. You took the risk, and you lost everything."

"No," his dad said, shaking his head sadly. "I didn't lose everything. When I was an adventurer, I was obsessive. All I cared about was making the next big capture, or getting big ratings for each show. That last season, it was really hard on your mother. We were fighting all the time. The truth is, she was just about to leave me. The accident . . . made me take stock. I realized that I wanted to be a better husband. A better father."

Karim didn't know what to say. He had never heard this side of events before. He stood in shocked silence.

"I'm not saying it was a good thing. But I have a good life, here with you and your mother. The accident took one life away from me but gave me another. I guess what I'm trying to say is . . . I don't regret any of it. The adventuring, the risks, the fame . . . and I don't regret ending up here, getting to stay with my wife and watching my son grow up every day."

His dad was saying good things, happy things, but somehow Karim could feel his eyes filling with tears, anyway.

"I'm proud of you."

"Thanks," Karim said. And then it just bubbled up out of him. "Dad . . . there's something I have to tell you. Sidesplitter, I—I actually stole it from you. A while before you gave it to me. We swapped it for Tommy's replica, that was what you gave me."

His dad paused for a long moment.

"Well, I suppose that was very clever," his dad said. "But

you shouldn't have taken it. Even though I always said it was going to be yours."

"I know."

His dad thought for a long moment, then shrugged. "I did dumber things than that when I was your age. I'd say you need to face some consequences, but from what I hear, your guidance counselor is taking care of that."

Karim hung his head.

"Look," his dad said. "Just . . . please don't lie to me, okay? Let's make a deal: You keep me in the loop, and I'll help you with your adventures."

Karim let out a breath that he didn't know he'd been holding. "Thanks, Dad. I'm really sorry I lied to you. It's a deal."

The Fang gave a grin. "You really got that jerk Tuckerville, though, didn't you?"

Karim laughed. "I still can't quite believe it."

His dad smiled. "I know more about monsters than just about anyone, except maybe that Mortimer fellow. You know, he was a real jerk to me once on an indigo leopard hunt in Malaysia," the Fang said, a wistful look coming over him. "Have I ever told you that story?"

As his dad launched into it, Karim was too relieved to follow all the details. He'd have to ask him to tell it again sometime when he could pay attention.

Tommy was walking down the hall to detention when Elissa jumped onto his back, in some mixture of a hug and an attempted tackle. Tommy almost stumbled, but he was a total beefcake, solid as a rock. He straightened up and patiently waited for Elissa to drop down.

"Dad just texted! We're both registered for Adventure Camp!" Elissa said, practically skipping down the hallway alongside her brother. "And it's just a few weeks away! Do you really think we'll get to see a real spike-horned ironhoof this year?"

Tommy grinned. "Who knows?! Maybe if they don't have one this year, I'll have to go out and catch one for you."

They reached the door to Room 208, aka the Sheriff's Lockup, as Karim liked to call it.

"Well, have fun in time-out, Tom-Tom!" Elissa said. "I'm going home to start packing!"

"Never too early, I guess," Tommy said, opening the door to the Sheriff's Lockup.

Once he was in detention, Tommy could barely sit still. It was just all too un-freaking-believable. A dragon! And an encounter with their archnemesis. And they had *won*. He could just sit there reimagining the whole thing over and over again.

Which was lucky, because they had been stuck in detention every day after school for the last two weeks. The Sheriff had even told him he couldn't bring in his usual after-school Brotein ("Weights: What comes down, must go up") shake. His body's Protein Power Potential Ratio—definitely a real and scientific thing—was totally crashing.

The Sheriff glared at him. "Shouldn't you be working, Tommy?"

She gave him an evil smile as he leaned down over his algebra homework, trying to make a show of calculating. She thought she had beaten them. She had been gloating for days.

The three of them sat in the front three desks of a classroom, the Sheriff only a few feet away at the teacher's desk. For the first few days they'd shared the room with Maria Struthers and Eddie Suarez, who were serving their much-delayed punishment for being caught skipping class to make out. At least those two lovebirds weren't in here passing each other mushy notes constantly.

Outside it was late afternoon, and the sound of kids practicing sports mixed with the distant roar of a lawn mower.

They were lucky there were only two weeks left in the school year, otherwise they might have gotten even more detention.

Sitting here in the fluorescent-lit classroom, those first-floor windows were like portals to another world, filled with mysteries and adventure. In here, it was just algebra equations and the smell of dry-erase markers. Karim actually seemed to be enjoying his algebra, in some odd way. Sicko.

Tommy slowly plodded through his work, pausing after each problem to rerun the highlight reel of their adventure in his mind.

A dark dungeon! Deadly ooze closing in! A daring escape on the back of a dragon!

They had posted the remaining videos. Even with their faces blurred out, they'd become huge hits. Every day after detention for the past week, the three friends had gathered around Spike's phone to review the latest comments and reaction videos.

And over the course of the past week, magic had happened. First on the adventure channels, there were confused reports that Mike Tuckerville had been arrested in Burbank, California. And then later, on every major news source— AppVenture headquarters raided by the Federal Monster Administration. Mike Tuckerville, being led out of a court-house in handcuffs. A judge ordering AppVenture to stop operating throughout the country. They replayed the video over and over again. Neither homework nor sleep happened that night for any of them.

Tommy continued to struggle with his homework and

had just started on his book report when the Sheriff's phone buzzed. She stepped into the hallway, talking loudly about the schedule for her son's Little League team.

Spike's new phone was immediately in her hand. Tommy wished he could join her, but his phone was a pile of wreckage lying in a park on the other side of town, and his family didn't have the money yet to get him a new one.

"Hey, we got our cabin assignments for Adventure Camp!" Spike said. "We're close to each other, at least."

Tommy grinned. Whatever happened in the last couple weeks of school, at least they had camp to look forward to. With the money that Spike's dad had gotten released, he had easily paid for both him and his sister.

"Sweet!" Karim said.

"Do you think they'll have the pegasus in the stables this year?" Tommy asked. He had been too scared to ride it two years ago, but this time he felt ready to try.

Outside, the Sheriff was ranting about how inconsiderate someone or other had been.

Spike sat bolt upright in her chair. "Um, guys . . . I just got a message from Mad Mackenzie."

"*The* Mad Mackenzie?" Tommy asked.

"What did she say?" Karim asked, straining to look over and see her phone. "What did she say?!"

Spike shook her head, appearing to be in a state of shock that was very rare for her. "She's just north of Burbank, hunting a pack of manic pixies," Spike said. "And she wants *our* help!"

"When?" Tommy asked.

Karim sighed. "Right now. If she's flushed them from their nest, she has until moonrise before they disappear for a year and a day."

They could hear the Sheriff walking up and down, loudly berating some poor parent.

Spike looked at the window, and Tommy followed her gaze. It was wide open, and they could easily fit through it, even with his muscular bulk.

"We already have detention to the end of the school year," Karim said. "What else could they do to us?"

Tommy grinned. A month ago, Karim would have been begging them to stay, and probably would have stayed behind even if Tommy and Spike went for it.

Spike shrugged. "Quite a lot, I'd imagine."

"Do we care?" Karim asked.

Tommy was already on his way to the open window, and he could hear his friends scrambling behind him.

Adventure was waiting for them.

ACKNOWLEDGMENTS

Creating a book is always an adventure, and the best adventures are faced with an adventuring party. I would like to offer not just gratitude but credit where credit is due to the team who helped make this idea a reality.

First and foremost, my editor, Orlando Dos Reis, has provided creativity, passion, thoughtfulness, and of course the push to just try harder. Supporting him, a whole team at Scholastic made this book happen, including production editor Josh Berlowitz and copyeditor Kerianne Steinberg. The striking cover and overall design are due to the illustrator Doug Holgate and designer Christopher Stengel. I also want to thank David Levithan and Zack Clark, who helped to make this project happen in the first place.

I would also like to thank my literary agent, Ammi-Joan Paquette, who was a true partner in guiding me through this process and being a tireless proponent of this project.

Outside the team of industry professionals, I need to thank Gabrielle Stein, Carrie Brown, Aenne Brielmann, and Rachel Sweeden, who read and gave valuable feedback to versions of this book as it was in progress. And Mallory Kass, Grace Kendall, Laura and Michael Bisberg, Laura Jean Ridge, and Nick Eliopulos, for both advice on specifics of this book and as well as being a writing support group for so many years. I would also like to acknowledge my dad,

Yorke Brown, who cheerfully ignores the fact that so many of my characters have issues with their fathers. At least the dads in this book are alive!

Beyond those who directly contributed to this book there are so many amazing people in my life who have been forced to listen to endless updates, complaints, and bragging as this book went from silly idea to finished product. I appreciate you, I love you, and I am forever grateful to have you in my life.

GAVIN BROWN is the author of *Josh Baxter Levels Up* and has written stories and designed games for the bestselling Spirit Animals and 39 Clues series. He is the creator of the highly rated iOS and Android game *Blindscape* and lives in a narrow apartment in New York City's East Village.